"Slipping into Sophie Mackintosh's fiction is as comforting as it is disquieting." —*The Boston Globe*

"Brilliant." —*The Brooklyn Rail*

"The novel reads like a mystery viewed through a haze of lust and misdirection. . . . [Readers will] find Mackintosh's incantatory prose as hypnotic as ever." —*Booklist*

"A master class in observation, of fracturing personalities but also in its tight and nuanced portrait of the rituals and minutiae of small-town life. Afterwards, you'll want to devour it all over again. 10/10." —*The Independent* (London)

"Mackintosh's top-notch phrasemaking and knack for forming uncanny images generate a baleful atmosphere of lust and dread in this splendidly peculiar tale." —*Daily Mail* (London)

"Intoxicating, sumptuous, and savage. . . . In Mackintosh's hands, the strange, compulsive machinations of desire become luminous and ghastly all at once." —Alexandra Kleeman, author of *Something New Under the Sun*

"*Cursed Bread* is a quietly rich maturation of Mackintosh's skill. . . . [She] has entered a brilliant new stage of writing." —*The Guardian*

Sophie Mackintosh

Cursed Bread

Sophie Mackintosh is the author of *Blue Ticket* and *The Water Cure*, which won the 2019 Betty Trask Award and was longlisted for the 2018 Man Booker Prize. In 2016 she won the White Review Short Story Prize and the Virago/*Stylist* short story competition. She has been published in *The New York Times*, *Elle*, and *Granta*, among other publications.

sophiemackintosh.co.uk

Cursed Bread

a novel

Sophie Mackintosh

VINTAGE BOOKS

A DIVISION OF PENGUIN RANDOM HOUSE LLC

NEW YORK

FIRST VINTAGE BOOKS EDITION 2024

Copyright © 2023 by Sophie Mackintosh

All rights reserved. Published in the United States by
Vintage Books, a division of Penguin Random House LLC,
New York. Originally published in hardcover in Great Britain
by Hamish Hamilton, an imprint of Penguin Books, a division of
Penguin Random House Ltd., London, in 2023, and subsequently
in hardcover in the United States by Doubleday, a division
of Penguin Random House LLC, New York, in 2023.

Vintage and colophon are registered
trademarks of Penguin Random House LLC.

The Library of Congress has cataloged the
Doubleday edition as follows:
Name: Mackintosh, Sophie, author.
Title: Cursed bread : a novel / Sophie Mackintosh.
Description: First edition. | New York : Doubleday, 2023.
Identifiers: LCCN 2022005436 (print)
Subjects: LCGFT: Novels.
Classification: LCC PR6113.A26493 C87 2023 (print) | DDC
823/.92—DC23
LC record available at https://lccn.loc.gov/2022005436

Vintage Books Trade Paperback ISBN: 978-0-593-46680-3
eBook ISBN: 978-0-385-54831-1

Book design by Cassandra J. Pappas

vintagebooks.com

Printed in the United States of America
10 9 8 7 6 5 4 3 2 1

For Edward

Nothing's gone, not really. Everything that's ever happened has left its little wound.

—SARAH MANCUSO

Cursed Bread

When I recall the first time I met Violet, it embarrasses me. I hold the memories up to the light and think—did it really happen like this? And even if it did, why not tell it differently? More generously? Why don't I pretend, even to myself? There's nobody left to know, nobody who could catch me out. I could say that she came in and took my hands in hers and looked into my eyes and said she always wanted a friend, a true friend, that she could see we were alike, with twin ravaging hearts under our ribs. My dour blouse could not conceal that from her. I could say that she picked me out of everyone in the town, was drawn along the sun-bleached stone of the pavements by hunger, by instinct, to where I had always stood, waiting.

I could say a lot of things, but perhaps it's best to be honest, now. I didn't sense her walking towards me on that chill morning in early spring, didn't notice her opening the door to the bakery. Her hair was dark and loose, spilling over her stiff white blouse and the lace at its collar. She hung behind the other customers, looking at the loaves stacked behind me one by one as if making an important decision. The other women in the shop greeted her.

Welcome, they said. We've been expecting you. She smiled at that, and I had to stop myself from brushing my hand against hers when I passed her the loaf she finally chose, but I couldn't say much to her, I was afraid of her. She thanked me and left, and through the window I saw her pause and open the paper bag for a second, as if she was considering tearing into the bread like a dog. But she didn't. She closed the bag, and then was gone. I stared after her until the next customer, I don't remember who, interrupted me, impatient for their breakfast. You've seen a ghost, they joked, snapping their fingers.

When I returned home later I found my husband asleep on our bed. He slept like a baby, insensibly, with his arms thrown out. I passed my hands over his body, not quite touching, along those splayed arms and along his legs, and finally, gently, lowered my palms to his chest. He was fully dressed. I climbed onto the bed, folded myself on top of him. His breathing changed but he refused to admit he was awake. Please, I asked him. I pressed my face into his neck. He was sweating. I wanted to put my hand over his mouth so he would stop pretending, but I knew he would rather suffocate than be caught. He kept his eyes closed. I batted at his arms, his cheeks, very lightly, then less lightly, then not very lightly at all.

I can admit that in those days I was sometimes jealous of the dough my husband put his hands into, worked so tenderly and tirelessly with, up to the elbows. I can admit now that his bread really was the best. There was such beauty in breaking it open hot from the oven and the steam pouring out, in feeling your appetite worrying at you and knowing it would soon be sated, the astonishing fact that, living as we did in this new time of peace and plenty, we might never have to feel truly hungry again. He was on a constant mission to perfect it. You might have said it was his life's work.

You might have said this not entirely seriously, but he was very serious about it. I was jealous too of the purity of his focus, the incremental moves towards one faultless loaf. But then what, when there was nothing left of the bread to improve? What then. Eat of it and be filled. Eat of it and be transformed. Eat of it and nothing changes. The almost-imperceptible recalibration of our desire, our satisfaction. Try again.

In the days that followed our first meeting, Violet haunted my thoughts. Would anyone believe me if I said I felt an intimacy with her even then? Would they believe that somewhere inside myself I knew what she would become to me? It was in the loaves I saved for her, whorled with flour. In the outfits I started to select the evening before, hanging on my cupboard door like bodies in the dark. In the slivers of information I prised out from her, prised out from the others. The matrons watched my little stabs at conversation when she came into the bakery, all my words running into each other. I was trying to be funny, showing off. We had lived in the same city for a while. We might have passed each other in the street. Through the slow afternoons I pictured her journey to us: a shining green car heading out of the city, stops on the way for her to look at the flowers in the fields. I started to wear a brooch that I had bought in that same city many years ago—pinning it to my chest like a signal. But her eyes upon it made it seem garish and unfashionable, she smiled at me without showing her teeth, and in a fit of rage I put the brooch in the bin when I closed the shop one day, sat behind the counter and cried. What have you got to cry about? my husband asked when I got home that night. He poured me a glass of milk. We live a very good life, he told me, cutting himself a thick slice of bread to eat with cheese, and it was true.

Every day I waited for her to come in, without knowing why,

without knowing what I would do. Finally, a couple of weeks after she arrived, though it felt like much longer, she put a hand in her pocket one morning and drew out a piece of paper, slid it across the counter. Blue ink, the handwriting of a man. We're having a party to meet everybody, she said. Won't you come along? She gave me the benediction of her smile. I felt my own lips respond involuntarily. I looked down at my hands, sticky, crumbed. We'll come, I told her.

The first time I saw the ambassador was at the lake. It was a small one, surrounded by trees, a little way out of the town. A hollowed-out copse of trees, the grass flattening vaguely into a path hardly wider than the tracks of a fox in the night. I would go there to swim just after dawn, to avoid the sinister children who threw clots of mud later in the day. Like sprites who might hold me under the surface and drown me at any moment. In the early morning I could slip my body into the world unnoticed, slip it into cold water, silken with mud, this body otherwise covered up with old cloth, apron, perfume, with layer upon layer. But that day a movement up ahead stopped me in the grass, made me press my body, still clothed, to a tree. A man, completely naked. I could see his clothes folded neatly on the ground behind him. He hadn't seen me. He hunched his shoulders up towards his ears, loosened them, stretched his arms out in front. It was quite cold. Perhaps he was gathering courage, I thought.

He walked into the cool water until he was up past his waist, raised his arms and pushed himself in. Until he surfaced, I held my breath. I would give anything to go back and see his body for the first time again. The shock of pale, unfamiliar flesh against green leaf, the hair wet against his head. Standing on the shore he had looked forbidding, even naked as he was, but the water washed something away from him. He became soft, glowing. He swam long and languid, and I thought of all the bodies I had known, how they had fitted or not fitted into mine, skin and breath on skin, and I lay down in the grass with the wings of the insects beating in my ears, so he wouldn't see me. I lay until the sound of the water stilled, until I was very sure that he was gone.

Dear Violet,

It has been a year now in this convalescent place by the sea. Elderly widows and tired mothers lounge in their deckchairs on the beach, or stroll the promenade; the white paint of the buildings blisters with salt. You would never willingly come somewhere like this, which perhaps is why I feel safe here. A year of the rain tapping on the window and the hotplate in the corner upon which I sometimes consider laying my palm, though the most I ever do is drop a strand of my hair to watch it curl and smoke. I walk up and down the concrete at the seafront counting the crabs that the seagulls have smashed on the floor, comforted by the horrible way the birds address their own hunger—almost inspired by it on some days.

The policemen sit with me in my room and I make them coffee in the two cups I own. They always want me to give my account of events. I should have some fun with it, tell them something different every time, but instead I don't tell them anything because there's nothing really to tell, because I want them to leave me alone. I make sure they cannot see my hands shaking. My hands are where it shows. Papery rucked skin. They don't do much of anything now, but the skin remembers, the body holds everything inside itself, the bones can still stiffen to claws. One of the policemen I think of as kind; I can tell he pities me. He says my name, then says it again—*Elodie*—and this makes the less kind policeman put his cup down so that it rattles. Sorry, sorry, I tell them. I'm listening, I tell them, though it's a lie. What I am really doing is watching the sand and rain blow against the window, and how the happy families run easily to safety, striped umbrellas held like weapons. Soon the policemen finish their coffee and they go. I won't talk, because the only real truth I could tell them is that sometimes there is a switch, and the world is turned upside down.

This is what it's like here: I do my penance. I slide my silver coins over the counter of the café and darn my stockings and at night my eyes are swollen little beads. I am a woman talking to myself alone in a room and I am a woman mute in a police station and I am a woman in a bar who nobody pays any attention to. I am a woman talking to you all of the time, wanting to feed words back to you, because you gave me so many, pushed them down my throat until I choked and enjoyed the choking, until the words spread through my blood, until I lit up. I think in another life I could have been a pathological liar, a professional one. I could have kept audiences rapt, could have talked my way out of and into things, rather than listening, watching, ruminating until I drive myself really mad. I always did imagine the two of you as characters from a story, after all.

O ur circle of women met at the lavoir once a week, Tues-days, heaving our bags of clothes. Whatever else happened in the town there would always be bread daily and me providing it, and there would always be the weekly circle of women to meet at the water, the patterns of light playing on our faces, for we always needed to eat and we dirtied our clothes with honest work, our lives ticking over. Sometimes, not very often, I found myself tied around the throat with a hot thread of panic at the inevitability of the days, as I watched the women who were my friends moving their hands through heavy swathes of wet cloth. Mme G, Mme A, the grocer's wife, Mme F and her daughter Josette, and the mayor's wife. We knelt down on the warm stone in our usual places around the shimmering square of water, and steadily we moved the suds across its surface. Ivy wound its way around the pillars holding up the roof that sheltered us from the rain when it fell, though it was very dry that year. I liked to listen to the birds nesting in its corners, tucked away in the gaps underneath the cracked red tiles.

That Tuesday I waited to see whether Violet would join us. Of course she did not, though I knew the mayor's wife had invited her. In her place, something better—Mme G, ancient and malevolent, was doing Violet's laundry. She shook out the bag and barked Look! as if she had dug up treasure, triumphant, white hair escaping from her navy-blue scarf. We left our own things then, gathered around her as she went through each scrap of fabric in turn. We passed them from hand to hand. A silken blue blouse. A dress of light primrose cotton. Knickers, ribboned, in black, in peach, in white, some of them spotted with blood, but we didn't recoil. We fingered the lace trims, the eyelets, the nightgown with pearlescent buttons all the way down the front. She's small, Mme F commented critically, holding up another dress to the light, this one deep rose, not a colour I would ever think to wear. Her daughter took the dress from her, stroked the fabric lovingly.

The grocer's wife was trying to have a baby. She told us about following the track of the moon, about the herbs her mother-in-law brewed for her, as we rinsed and wrung. She had to eat offal to conceive a boy, she had to be willing at all times, even when the grocer was drunk, even when he berated her for their difficulties. She had to remain calm and superstitious, alive to the world and all its miracles. I'm praying to the Madonna, she said, pious. Try praying to someone who isn't a virgin, said Mme A darkly, and all of us except the grocer's wife laughed. But even her predicament was not enough to distract them from Violet for long. I listened to their rumours, my eyes on my own clothes, heavy with water.

She orders her groceries in hampers from the city.
She bathes in milk and rose petals.
She sits out on the balcony all night, doesn't sleep.
The ambassador rescued her from an asylum.
She was a cabaret singer.
She was a whore.

She invited me to a party, the grocer's wife volunteered, almost guiltily.

Me too, I said.

Mme G lowered herself into a crouch, with difficulty, next to the water. You must tell us what you find out, she said. We're counting on you young ones. With a leisurely, graceful violence, she hit a white bed sheet against the surface of the water and left it to soak. The grocer's wife smiled at me. I would always be one of them, nobody looking at me could deny it. With teeth hard in my mouth, the curve of my long neck, and my hair strong, bleached every four weeks like clockwork, my head tipped over the sink as I sluiced burning ammonia down the drain. My feet were flat. My hips were wide. I was bloody all the way through. I didn't have to say it out loud; the women nodded their heads. They understood that much, at least.

When I stepped into Violet's house for the first time, I felt something glassy and sharp high in my abdomen. It was a house that had been empty most of the year, tucked away down a backstreet, and now it was full of lilies and irises, their petals cool and sweet, and lit up with dozens of candles. She must have spent all day arranging it. My eyes darted, taking everything in. Despite the flowers, despite the floorboards waxed to an exacting shine, I fancied I could smell the damp that still lingered underneath, even the acrid smell of mice, and this pleased me. I spotted the grocer's wife and the mayor's wife with their husbands, across the room, wearing dresses I knew were their best, but which seemed old-fashioned even to me—too long, too shabby, too loose on the waist. On the other hand, Violet was overdressed in a way that would have been laughable on anybody else—in black velvet, a tight diamond necklace, both too grand for the occasion, her dark hair swept up.

Have a drink, she ordered, raising her hand, drifting away before I could reply.

The drawing room was soon full of blue smoke. I escaped my

husband and wandered for a while before settling near the door. Across the hallway I could see another open door, a kitchen, and inside Violet was peeling cheeses out of their waxed paper and dropping them carelessly onto a large blue-and-white-striped platter. After a while the ambassador slipped out into the hall, nodding at me as he passed. He joined his wife in the kitchen and I watched him stroke her cheek, and she turned to him. He moved to kiss her, her mouth tipped up to his, and his hands went from her face, suddenly, to her throat. The glassy pain returned. Still kissing her, he pressed harder, harder still—he was strangling her, I thought in disbelief, he was strangling her right there. He would take off her entire head. I looked over my shoulder at the rest of the room, everybody oblivious to what was happening just a few metres away, and then I stepped into the hall. But I blinked and they were apart, it was the smoke, an optical illusion, they were laughing happily together. I turned hastily back into the drawing room.

They came back into the room together, and I watched as they moved in a sort of choreography, wordlessly separating and circling the space. Violet dropped in on a conversation between the butcher, the grocer and their wives, but didn't speak, just listened. I watched her tilt her head to the side and smile with her lips, watched her eyes move to each of their faces in turn, watched the men in the group straighten up and heard their voices grow louder, each of them competing to talk. Her eyes looked up and over them, briefly, and I followed her gaze to the ambassador, standing with the blacksmith and the owner of the local bar, and his eyes answered hers. Soon they moved on, graceful, first her and then him, cutting through the small crowd. The wife of the mayor had found me and was talking, something about her son. I just smiled as she moved her hands around. Across the room the grocer's wife was talking to my husband, making him laugh as he examined a table of hors d'oeuvres. I wondered whether he was drunk. He was usually a big and silent rock of a man, his features oddly pretty for somebody of his size, with long eyelashes and soft lips; I paused to admire him, briefly, like he belonged to someone else. The mayor's wife excused herself, and I walked over to join my husband.

Soon it was our turn. I saw Violet turn towards us and I resolved not to be deferential, not to fawn like the others did, but it was difficult to know how to arrange myself instead. Normally I was bright and bartering, always something to offer, but what was there to offer this immaculate stranger? She introduced herself to me as if she didn't recognize me from the bakery at all. Hello, I'm Violet, she said.

Elodie, I replied, wrong-footed.

The introductions moved around our small circle and I was startled to realize the ambassador had joined us, appearing noiselessly at my side.

Violet moved nearer to the table and her hand hovered over a piece of baguette smeared with tomato, then dropped. My husband definitely was drunk, I could tell when he started to enthuse about bread. He asked Violet where she had bought the bread for the party, how she had prepared it. He was very pleased when she said, It's your bread, of course; I was pleased too when her eyes flicked to me as she said it. So she does remember me, I thought. This led my husband into a speech about his own techniques, one I had heard many times before, and about the noble pursuit of the perfect loaf. His arms went everywhere. I felt a violent mix of distaste and affection. The ambassador was humouring him, which my husband didn't seem to notice. There are artificial additives in the flour in America, the ambassador offered. That's what makes our bread so white. I ate oysters wetly from a plate of melting ice, cool salt on my tongue and the sting of the lemon, and when nobody was looking I slipped one empty shell into my bag, then another, and then I knew I was drunk too, though I hadn't even finished my second glass of wine.

The grocer's wife excused herself with a smile, escaping my husband's lecture. Come and sit down, Violet said then, which she had said to nobody else, as far as I had seen. It felt like a golden light had been shone upon us. She led us to the velvet chairs at the back of the room and the four of us sat, our knees pressed close together. So you two, my husband said, looking at them. Newest members of the town. Why come here?

Work, the ambassador explained simply. A government project, a kind of survey.

We recoiled in respect. He took a swallow of his wine.

It's important to learn more about the real people of this country. To truly get to know them, the citizens who make it what it is. The people like you, he said. He gestured around the room. I moved my eyes and saw the others taking no notice of us. My husband gave me a look, eyebrows lifted slightly. *What next*, he seemed to be asking. I had never known him to be curious. My mouth was heavy. The shadows on the wall moved, candles casting them unevenly. The ambassador had his hands on his thighs, pressed down, he was looking at Violet.

How did you meet? I asked. Violet crossed her legs, alert, leaned forward a little.

My sister's wedding, the ambassador said, still watching his wife.

Yes, Violet said. I'm an old friend of his sister from school. She named a school I didn't recognize, but I murmured encouragingly as if I did. She smiled. I was at the wedding with a group of other girls we'd gone to school with, and I was having a terrible time, she said.

I saved you, the ambassador said. He must have been anticipating his cue, coming in at the perfect moment. The ease of a story told again and again and again, not yet tired of. The party around us was quite loud, music playing from a gramophone in the opposite corner, a woman singing mournfully. I had to listen carefully, to watch closely as their mouths moved.

Yes, she said again. She was always saying it to him   *yes, yes, yes*—as if desire was only ever so simple, so affirmative. There was a man who kept trying to make conversation with me, she continued, and it was so boring, and then this man—here she tapped him lightly on his arm in its fine covering of dark twill—this man, this stranger, came along and took hold of me and pretended to be my husband.

I thought on my feet, he said. I could just see your lovely face, and how unhappy you were to be trapped in conversation with him. I had to do something.

How did the other man react? my husband asked.

He took it in his stride, Violet said, holding his gaze. Wouldn't you?

I'd have put up a fight, my husband said, smilingly, to let them know he meant no harm. The ambassador laughed, to let him know no harm was done.

Anyway, he steered me away, and we drank a lot of champagne together instead, Violet said. She was laughing too by this point.

And we went outside onto a little balcony so we could talk without all the noise of the party, and out of nowhere we heard a great commotion, down on the street below.

Here she paused for effect.

What was it? I asked, with the appropriate animation.

There was a murder taking place, the ambassador said.

He said it very calmly—so calmly that for a moment I thought I must have been mistaken. Violet nodded. She reached over to refill our glasses and a droplet ran down the bottle. She caught it before it hit the table, put her finger in her mouth as if it were a drop of blood.

A murder, she said. We didn't really see anything, she added quickly, only some blood on the pavement, or maybe it was just rain, it had rained earlier in the night. And some blood on the dress of a woman, she was screaming, but she wasn't the one being murdered. Maybe she was even just passing by, at the wrong time.

How did you know? my husband asked. He was rapt, his mouth was open. Did you phone the police?

The ambassador took a long inhale on his cigarette. We didn't bother, we didn't want to get involved, he said. We didn't know it was a murder until days afterwards, you see, when it was in the paper. We just thought it might have been a lovers' quarrel, or a fight.

We weren't sure it was blood, Violet interrupted. It could have been wine, it was hard to tell, so dark down there, and maybe it was raining again by then, the details get away from me, it all happened so quickly.

We didn't understand what we were seeing, but we knew that we felt lucky not to be them, the ambassador said. Safe, up there, on the balcony. In love.

You weren't in love with me then, you barely knew me, she said, shoving him delightedly.

I was, I was, he insisted, putting his hand upon his chest. They looked into each other's eyes, too deeply; it made me feel uncomfortable.

You should lead with the murder, not the wedding, my husband said, oblivious to them. Isn't that the better story?

I prefer the element of surprise, Violet replied.

Maybe we'll try your way when we tell it next time, the ambassador said.

I felt left out, picked up a cigarette from the packet lying on my husband's lap   slowly, with ceremony. The ambassador broke away from looking at his wife and leaned from his seat to give me a light, almost kneeling in front of me as he cupped the flame with his hands, and met my eyes, and our faces were illuminated with dizzying possibility for one brief second. The sweet click of the lighter. She was watching me lazily, I was no threat to her, matron-adjacent with my hair falling down from where I had pinned it into submission. The ambassador returned to his seat, and without warning she slithered down from her chair as if falling, ungracefully, but catching herself softly on the shining floor. She leaned her head against his knee, and he gripped her face with one hand, fingers under her chin. He lit his own cigarette and then passed it to her, allowed her one breath only, then took it back.

We met on the beach, many years ago, I said.

At my side, the slight stiffening of my husband's body as I blew out smoke.

We met in the water, actually, I said. Technically.

Paddling? asked Violet, as I considered my options, where to go next, the movement of the body next to me, which I didn't dare look at.

No, she was swimming. She swam out too far, my husband said, before I could answer.

I did look at him, then. I looked sharply at him and saw the smoothness of his face, the easy smile, I saw him take out his own cigarette from the blue packet on his lap, and it was my turn again.

That's right, I said. I was distracted by the feel of the water, and when I looked back then, the shore seemed miles away. The current was stronger than I had anticipated. I thought I was going to die.

I gave out a small laugh to dilute the melodrama. I had over-stepped, perhaps. Violet watched me. My husband remained silent, he wasn't watching me, he seemed lost in thought, as if remembering it alongside me.

Probably I was in no danger, I told them. But it was frightening. I turned and tried to swim back, and then I saw another head rise above the waves.

You, Violet said, pointing at my husband.

Me, he said, after a small hesitation. Yes, me. I had seen her on the beach and noticed her at once.

At last he looked at me. He put the hand not smoking the ciga-rette on my knee and it felt like the most intimate thing we had done in months. I refused to be undone, remained focused—on the couple watching us, the smoke, the fingers of the ambassador which seemed to be pressing harder into the tender skin of Violet's jaw, and the sound of the party around us, which had grown more clamorous.

I thought she was beautiful, he said.

My husband's hand on my knee gripped me the way the ambassador gripped Violet's face. *Harder*, I thought, but this wish was either not transmitted, or transmitted and not obeyed.

She was reading her book, my husband continued. She hadn't seen me watching. When she went into the water I followed her out of curiosity. I realized we were going out too far, and I saw her realize it too.

But you pulled her to safety, Violet said. Or else you both died there, and you are apparitions before us now. But you seem real to me.

My husband looked to me. I was electrified by his fluency, the words that came out of his mouth. I felt myself grow wet under my faded dress, cut too high at the throat.

He reached out his hand, I said. And I almost remembered the salt sting, the way the water lapped cold into my mouth. I felt myself there. He pulled me through the waves, I said. He's strong, from kneading bread his whole life.

Here I paused to roll up the sleeve of his shirt, carefully. He made no move, he let me do it, like it was a part of the story I had told many times before. Violet and the ambassador squeezed his forearm, gravely, in turn. Violet lingered slightly longer than she had to, the pale manicured tips of her fingernails almost digging in, and met not my husband's eyes, but my own. Maybe I had elevated myself to the level of a threat after all, maybe she had sensed something upon me. When she sat back on the floor the ambassador resumed his strange grip on her jaw, tighter still, the angle tense as if he could twist her neck right around with the slightest extension of the gesture—another optical illusion like the one in the kitchen, though she seemed very comfortable like that.

What happened next? she asked.

I pulled her to safety, my husband said, warming up further. I told her to hang on to me, and then I swam.

I hung on for dear life, I said. The current seemed so strong, by then.

You were just tired, my husband said.

He motioned swimming with his arms. I could feel the cold blue water around me, feel the smooth skin of his back as I clutched him, as we were propelled onwards.

We made it onto shore, and then the lifeguards checked me over, I said. I was sick on the sand, I was embarrassed when he saw.

You shouldn't have been, it was nothing, my husband said.

He bought me an orange juice, I said. He asked if he could see me again.

We were running out of steam, had reached the limits of our imaginations. I could see my husband losing interest.

Were you in love? Violet asked, leaning closer. Did it throw you both into love?

It threw me into something, he said.

He looked into my eyes in an imitation of the way they had looked into each other's, convincing enough to an unsuspecting witness. To know it was an imitation was my punishment. But then we were interrupted by the mayor's wife knocking over a candle, setting an arrangement of dried roses aflame, and I was glad. We all ran to investigate, but there was no real sense of peril. The grocer put it out neatly with a napkin-clothed hand, his wife throwing a glass of water over the scene for good measure. Soon there was just a wet, scorched circle in the tablecloth, which Violet poked as if it were an eye. It was time for the mayor's wife to be carted off in her husband's arms, a bundle of limbs, whimpering. In the commotion my husband took my arm. He put his mouth to my ear. What happened there? he asked, and I didn't know what to tell him. With his face so close to mine I wanted to kiss him on his red mouth, or on the little damp curls of his forehead, but he turned away before I could, so there was only the white-clothed back of him.

We continued shuffling through the party for a while, all the people we had known for years, my husband topping up our glasses every time I took a sip, before I understood both Violet and the ambassador had disappeared. Nobody missed me as I left the room, went into the darkened hallway with its tall candles in a brass holder in the corner, the sound of the rain coming down. The kitchen door was open and it was dark inside, so they could not be in there. They must be upstairs, I realized, and without thinking I began to climb, as if their bodies were pulling at mine, slowly, I couldn't see much, only the swimming orange ghost of light behind me, and then as I climbed higher I could see a different light, a thin bright slice of it in the corridor ahead. I stood before this slice of light, which led to a door ajar, I trembled before it, unseen in the darkness. I pressed my body to the wall. Their voices murmured, the shapes of their bodies intruded on the piece of light. One or both of them were pacing, bodies circling.

You are not a well person, I heard the ambassador say, or thought I did.

Look after me, then, she said. I discovered if I moved a little closer to the door I could see more than I had first assumed, I could see her in profile sitting on the bed, her hands crossed on her lap, very still.

You make that very difficult, I heard him say. He was not quite in my line of sight, he must have been standing directly in front of her. My mind filled in the gaps. There was a sound as if he moved to the floor—*prostrated himself* was the phrase that came into my mind. Her hands remained still, perhaps he was clutching at her ankles.

It's the baker. Do you want to fuck him? he asked. The ambassador came into view then, his head suddenly appearing above her knees. I froze, worried I might be seen even in the darkness of the corridor, but his gaze was focused on her. He rested his head in her lap, cheek to fabric. I know you want to fuck him, he said.

You're out of your mind, she said, disappointing me. I watched as she took his head in her hands as if to draw him nearer, to kiss and caress him, but instead she seemed to push him slightly away. Absorbed, I pulled unthinkingly at my earlobe, and with horror I felt the cheap blue bead from my earring break away and fall to the floorboards. Lowering myself gently to my knees I swept my hands across the floor in the darkness, slowly, slowly, but I could not find it.

The ambassador was still talking. I saw you looking at him, he was saying, shaking her off, catching her wrist. I saw you looking at the bread.

What about me, I thought, but they didn't mention me at all, not then and not later, maybe not at all.

I didn't eat it, she said, calmly, like this strange conversation was one they had daily. You saw me, I didn't eat it.

You wanted to eat it, and you wanted to fuck him, he said. I can smell it on you, he said. Perhaps he gripped her by the ankles here instead, I can't be sure.

But I didn't, she said, and then her voice was higher than it had been, almost shrill, though that's not really a quality I associate with her then or now, so sometimes I think I've misremembered. A puling alarm-filled tone, like a child's.

The thought of her undoing the buttons of my husband's white shirts excited me, the deft movement of her fingers, those fingers which were now in the mouth of the ambassador, as if he would bite them off one by one. His lips were soft and obscene around them, up to the knuckle.

Releasing her fingers, gleaming wet, he said, Tell me you'll do anything I say.

Yes, she said. I will.

If you eat the bread, you'll die, he said, and it sounded more like a caress than a threat, and his face was pressed into the fabric of her skirt again so the words came out muffled, indistinct. The statement made no sense, but it filled me with an electric dread.

Yes, she said again, trance-like. I will.

He sat back with sudden grace, and then his hand at the end of his sleeved arm, almost disembodied in the darkness, reached out to clutch at her throat again. His hands were large enough that the tips of his fingers reached round to the back of her neck. But she laughed at him, then sighed with what seemed like relief, no longer shrill. I wanted to fling open the door. Should I get someone, I thought, knowing that I would not. Her body went limp. There was a soft touch on my arm, and I turned to see my own husband, not looking at me, but peering past me to the sliver of light and the bedroom. His face was implacable. We watched and listened together, his head turning to catch more of the sounds they made, the sighs which seemed close to weeping.

We walked back through silent streets, not touching. At home I washed the oyster shells and put them in my jewellery box alongside my broken earring, and then I turned to face my husband over our bed.

What's your first memory of me? I asked him. The real one.

He shrugged. It must have been in the café, he said. I don't really remember.

He turned away from me to pull off his clothes, and I did the same. Finally, finally, he lay on top of me, after turning out the light. It was mournful. He licked his palm and touched himself in the dark. My hands curled loosely at his back, and I wondered if he was thinking of them, if he was imagining I was Violet, if he was thinking of a strange woman being pulled by him through an ocean. I experimented with moving, with making a little breathless noise, but when I did he stiffened, threatening to break whatever rare spell had compelled us. Instead, then, I turned inside my body and pretended to myself that I was her.

This was my first clumsy fantasy of them, and maybe love began for me here. I was no longer me, but instead was her—languid and perfumed and undressed with care, diamonds shone in my ears, there was a man prostrating himself on the floor in front of me, gripping my ankles as if to pull me closer to him, as if to hold me firmly in place. My husband's juddering motions told me he was close. Stay with me, I told myself, willing pleasure, trying to find it. I clasped my hands together, so lightly, holding him very carefully as if he might break. Stay with me.

My husband was right — we met in a café, where I worked at the time. The first time I laid eyes on him, he hadn't seen me yet. His hair was lighter then, and he had more of it, long across his forehead. He was wearing a blue shirt, he seemed very solemn and kept looking around. He was with an older man, who I thought, correctly, was his father, and this man was counting out coins onto the table. In the years after, I grew to treasure the memory of that moment, of seeing my future before I knew what it was, seeing the pair of them before they were my husband and my father-in-law, when they were just two strangers. I swiftly made evaluations—they were not well off, they had to count their coins out for breakfast, they might be on holiday, or in the city for work—and they reminded me of my own family, whom I never thought of if I could help it. This filled me with both sentimentality and unease, set my heart's scene, because sometimes we return to what we recognize, whether we want it or not.

The tablecloth was white but stained, and I had flipped it over when I laid the table so nobody would see the marks. I stalled; I had to go and take their order, but I was tired that day and didn't feel like talking. Every day I went to work and wondered if it would be the day something or someone walked through the door and changed my life. It could be him, I thought from across the room as I worked up the energy, or maybe I only think that now, retrospectively, to give the memory gravitas. The floor was green linoleum, the menu was spread in front of him although he wasn't reading it, the waiter drying dishes at the sink with a red cloth, though they were smeared and not properly clean, wiping them once, then again. But I did walk over in the end and ask them what they wanted, and he looked up at me and ordered a boiled egg and bread. Black coffee. I didn't know that he would become something to me and that that something would change with time, would grow dearer and then less dear, less strange and then more so, the memory of the old affections jostling for space with the new hurts, incredible, recriminatory. The egg came peeled and he opened up his bread and with no self-consciousness put the egg on top, over-salted it, and mashed it very methodically with his fork, as if it was something he did every morning. I watched him do it as I took the order of another table. By the time he was satisfied enough to eat you could hardly tell what was egg and what was bread.

He came in the café again the next day without his father and sat at the same table. He was shy, he was from elsewhere, I liked his long tapping hands, I liked his light hair, I didn't like that he had to count his coins, but he didn't count them that day, so maybe I forgot. He just ordered coffee this time, one cup, then another, waiting to talk to me. And I felt more like talking that day, I had been thinking about the eviscerated egg and was disappointed when he didn't order one, and he never ate one like that again, not to my knowledge, as if it was a rare treat or temporary affectation or both, though I waited, hopeful, every time.

On the cool blue morning after the party, I woke up with my husband, lay there with my eyes pressed shut. Let him suspect nothing, I thought. Let him suspect me marble-like as a corpse. He was buttoning his shirt. He made no noise beyond the exhalation of breath, no little utterances of frustration or song. With my eyes still shut I heard him fetch a glass of water. I could not hear the swallow of water catching in his throat but I could imagine his hand lifting the glass, clenching around it and then releasing, leaving it on the table for me, to wash up or to drink from too, which is what I did when I heard the door open then shut. It was hard to find the exact place on the glass where his lips had been, though I inspected the rim, I made my best guess and put my lips there too. I have always been a sort of archivist, glutting myself on what has been left behind.

I dressed quickly in the previous day's clothes and made my way down to the dark street. My husband was ahead of me, and he suspected nothing. From a distance I appraised the way he moved when nobody else was around, but could detect no difference, no simmering sense of anger or of wonder or private joy. I was disappointed, but also I thought maybe I was too far away to see the signs, that there could still be some mystery there to excavate, if I only looked close enough. Was he feeling cheerful, or was it just the unthinking movement of his body? It was hard to know, it was a failure in me that I didn't know. It felt good to name these shames, salving to admit them to myself. He disappeared into the bakery. I waited in the cold with my arms around myself.

When I was sure he was downstairs I walked through the side alley to the back, stepped around the bins to the low, narrow window which gave onto the cellar, and then on my hands and knees I got down into the dirt to see what my husband was doing. He was wet with sweat already, wearing one of his usual heavy linen shirts. I knew exactly the texture of these shirts and how they smelled pressed up to my face, how they felt when I was searching for some kind of evidence, the kind of evidence any wife would look for. I thought to myself how the worst I had done really was not any of the little betrayals but in murdering my marriage with familiarity, and it was unfair because that is only what marriage demands, the careful establishing of familiarity in order to be able to live your life the next day and the next and the next.

He shaped the dough and put it in the pans, efficient, balletic. It felt like I was watching something that should not be seen, but then there was nothing really to see. It was a disappointment and a relief. His hands worked smoothly and unthinkingly, he was unreadable, which maybe meant he was happy, that he wanted for nothing. And this made it worse, the idea that he wanted for nothing, and it was just me who was alone with my desire like a ragged hole in my chest. Watching him made me want him, watching him as another might see him, with his good strong arms and his hands that patted, shaped, stretched, his hands everywhere and easy, his hands not on me.

The things that keep us alive are not very often erotic, but it's all right because there is so much left that is. The rising dough; the glimpses just out of sight promising something better, something yet to come. What if Violet could see me low to the ground, with the palms of my hands and my bare knees, my dress pulled up, filthy? She would nod with interest, I decided then. She would understand the desire to watch, to see, would not find me pathetic, even when I discovered that there was nothing for me there.

Dear Violet,

What do I do all day, you must wonder, V? How do I fill my hours without you? I picture you picturing me. Do you see me in your mind's eye, reeling with desperation? Do you see me with pity? Do you see me taking my stupid little walk in the morning, along grey pebble, wet sand, concrete promenade? I try to go further each time, even if only a step. One day I'll end up on another coast, another edge of this country. I'll be the miracle woman who walked until her feet were worn to the bone. Perhaps you can walk a thing away, or walk yourself away, wear yourself into a slip of sinew. The trick is forgetting for one moment and then forgetting for another moment and then look, the moments run together like a string of beads, and there is heartbreak in the forgetting of heartbreak, in the forgetting of pain, which returns bright and pulsing regardless of the seconds it has been put aside. Do not leave me here, it tells you. Pain becomes an animal, walking at your side. Pain becomes a home you can carry with you.

If it rains I wrap myself in oilcloth. I don't mind my hair dripping down my neck if I can look at the sea, the waves which don't end and will never end. There's no arguing with a tidal pattern. It comes in, and then it goes out again. One step after another.

After the walk I take my coffee, read the paper. They know me at the café—if I miss a day they ask after me—though I don't know what they say about me among themselves. Afterwards I go and buy food. I go to the bakery every day. With an expert's eye I'm critical of the croissants, the baguette's crust. *Body of Christ*. It took me a while to go in there, but what else was I going to do? Who did I think I was? Do you lay bread on your tongue and think of me, Violet, do you swallow it like a sacrament, do you still get down on your knees? Is there someone on their knees before you, clutching at your ankles, murmuring words for whatever ghost is watching at the door to overhear and remember?

I buy the bread and rip it with my hands in the street, the way I thought you might do once. I break it with such violence and then I take the first bite there, like marking a kill. In the evening I take my dinner at one of the red-lit restaurants near the pier, the lights of the boats shining out from the sea to me. Or maybe just a snack in the bar, olives rammed on sticks, cheese. Maybe a man to buy me a drink and come back with me in the dark. In between, the remembering. Some days I try so hard to remain focused on the routine, grimly greeting the next thing as it comes, the newsprint on my fingers, the bitter rush of the coffee, the wind in my face like a slap.

A confession, Violet—last night I dyed my hair black like yours. I suppose I was moved by the same impulse that sometimes leads me to think I am becoming you, that we commune uneasily across the distance. I am even becoming thin like you, though I don't wear it well. With the mirror propped in front of the basin I painted the dye on, blurring darkly around my hairline. Hours after I rinsed it out there were still smudges of grey around the porcelain. My hands ran over my new hair, which felt more lustrous than before, but when I saw my pale face in the mirror the spell was broken. Transformation is a membrane-fragile magic, easily disturbed by a breath. I knew the grey would soon come through at the roots. Nevertheless I put on your old lipstick, lined my lips first with my own pencil to avoid the bleeding out from the edges that you were always prone to.

Today I was in the café and I noticed two lovers sitting at the table next to mine. They held hands under the table rather than openly, and their fingers were restless, twining and untwining. If I really were you, Violet, what would I have done? This is a question I ask daily. If I were you, they would have been the ones taking furtive glances at me, they would have forgotten all about each other. Or if I were you, I might not care or even notice whether they saw me or not. But I am me, ever gleaning crumbs to feed upon, so I listened closely while feigning nonchalance.

They didn't know each other well. One of the couple, a girl with dark red hair, described her mother, who she lived with in a small house in the next town. She can't see me with you, the girl said, urgently. She would run in here and she would hit you around the head. She'll be wondering where I am right now. But my intentions are quite innocent, her companion replied. Meanwhile under the table his hand quickened, became more decisive. His thumb stroked the palm of her hand, his grip became closer, and her hand, initially a squirming thing, relaxed or succumbed to the new pressure.

The waiter brought me my coffee, and I smiled, and put a sugar cube from the little red lacquer bowl in my mouth when he was not looking. You would not do this either.

It was the turn of the boy to give an account of himself, so he talked about his sister, his only remaining family, who had moved to the city in the north. His ordinary words didn't match up with the action of his hands, both of which were by then holding that one of hers under the table, so tightly it must have been uncomfortable. One hand drew its nails lightly over her palm as if divining a future. She works in a place like this, he said. He dug his nails in then, pulled her hand closer to him—she winced, but she didn't look away from his moving mouth. Everybody else died, he told her, without elaborating. She stiffened, made to pull her hand back, but he wouldn't let go, in fact he pressed harder. When he did release his grip both her hands scudded to her lap at once as if thrown there, but apart from that she didn't move, her eyes remained on his face. I wondered what answering account of herself she would give, what reciprocal tragedy to reveal. Whatever she chose would bind them with uneasy and involuntary intimacy, and he must have been aware of this as a mode of seduction, because his hands under the table gave the game away.

Sometimes in the last year I have been known to tell people *I am from the town where the man cut out his own heart*, and I hate myself for invoking this, glancing off the spectacle, borrowing its trappings as a mode of seduction. But sometimes I just want to be witnessed. Sometimes seduction is the last thing on my mind.

It was easy to see how the red-headed girl would give herself over to him that afternoon in his dark room, heavy with the smell of mildew and salt, and then she would return to the house she shared with her mother, matching red hair, the woman waiting up to slap her face until her mouth was full of blood. That's what you do with a daughter, especially a bad one, and they're all bad ones, stricken with their own loveliness, stricken with their own doom. But it's all conjecture. I didn't stay to hear her speak, only catching those low first words that capture and portend all badness, *When I was younger.*

The children of the village liked to come into the bakery, knowing I would give them something to eat, even if I pretended at first I wouldn't. It was a game we played, me being stern as they laughed, shooing them away from the trapdoor that led to the hot cellar. They were afraid of the cellar and fascinated by it. If you go down there my husband will bake you into a loaf, I threatened. I was not always in the mood for their small darting movements, but I always allowed them in. Easy to be generous when there was so much to be given. I would wag my finger at them, then present sugared bread from behind my back. I was so very bored.

A few weeks after the party, I hadn't spoken to Violet again. Once or twice I glimpsed her through the window, passing on the other side of the street, or seated beside her husband at church, and I would feel a pulse of something run through me. Just as I was starting to wonder if she would ever come in again, she turned up at the bakery one afternoon, right before I closed it. I'll wait, she said, I wanted to talk to you. She slipped behind the counter without asking and sat on a stool like a child as I dealt with the last customers. They paid and watched her. She waved at them. How are you? she said. They murmured and left. I locked the door and came back to her. My cheeks grew warm. You're so red, she told me. Have you been in the sun? She put the cool back of her hand to my forehead. Not feverish, she said. Not as far as I can tell. The softness of her touch was as unexpected as a blow.

Did you enjoy the party? she asked me. Did you have a nice time?

Was she laughing at me, I wondered, growing warm again. I smiled tightly.

Can I offer you something to eat, I said. There's plenty left.

She didn't protest. I retrieved a small brioche from the display case, went down to the cellar to fetch a plate, came back up and set it in front of her. She looked at it placidly as if it were a rock.

A napkin, I said out loud, finding one in the drawer beneath the counter and laying it on her finely clothed knees, the billowing cotton skirt. I patted the napkin smooth with new boldness, as if her body belonged to me.

She cupped the brioche in her hands and smoothed her thumbs over the top, dug them in suddenly, breaking through to the soft belly of the bread.

It's very kind of you, but I'm not hungry, she said. She pulled it in half, slowly, then ripped each half into smaller pieces.

Don't think me rude, she said, ripping each piece smaller. Some of the crumbs fell to the floor.

What about this, I said, reaching for a knife and sawing off the end of a loaf, putting it on the plate before she could protest. There's jam, I said. There's butter, but it doesn't need it.

She picked at the crust with her fingernails. A little dark part of me wanted to thrust it between her lips, lodge it deep in her mouth, her throat. *Eat it*, I willed her. All through the day I had been eating that same bread, morsel by morsel, ripped off and chewed. It sat in my stomach, it seemed to grow, to weigh heavier on me.

Not this either, she said. It's nothing personal.

With the same measured gestures as before she ripped up the bread, more falling to the floor this time. She looked at me with no shame.

If you eat the bread, you'll die. I would not ask, I refused to ask. I reached up to the shelf behind me and took down a beautiful green apple which I had been saving for myself, took up the same knife I had used for the bread even though it was the wrong kind, and cut the apple into slices. One paper-thin slice in the palm of my hand, held out to her, you could see the pink of my skin through it, you could see the creased lines of my future. She accepted this. She lifted it to her mouth and her little pink tongue licked it, like a cat, and then she took a single bite. It was so wonderful to see that I forgot about the bread. She put the rest of the apple slice on the plate. It bore the mark of her lipstick, her teeth.

That's enough, she said. I'll see you soon. She stood up and walked out of the door without looking back.

I ate what was left of the apple, including the slice she had half eaten. I took the dustpan and the brush and I swept up the crumbs of the bread, muddied with dust, but even though the idea occurred to me I didn't put them in my mouth. I was not that far gone. Nobody, at the beginning, believes they will debase themselves for love. Nobody believes in anything else but joy.

Dear Violet,

You never asked me what it was like to spend my life listening as other people spoke. You never asked what it was like to hold those words inside me, to decide what to share, what to insinuate, but mainly what to keep for myself, these glowing and sordid little secrets that sustained me.

An affair, she told me, that's why she walks around the town with her eyes half-closed.

Sickness, he said, she doesn't have long to live now.

There's no more baby.

My son grows worse by the day.

I'm in love, she told me.

I'm in love, he told me.

I'm waiting for her to die.

I'm leaving, he told me (but did not leave, nobody leaves).

I need somebody who can sort it out.

Don't tell anyone, she told me.

Don't tell anyone.

It felt like I was the only one who could really see the ways our lives crossed over those of one another, tensile pieces of string prone to breaking. It was complicated, but reassuring too.

Our priest used to glare at me in the street, like I was his competition. In confession, there was never anything for me to tell him except *waste, Father*, when we had to throw away bread—once only, *sinful thoughts, Father*, long before you arrived in the town, just another bad season, with the rain coming down that time, hard enough to drown the rats in the sewers and wash them up bloated at the side of the river. That summer I felt desire with no distinct object or directive, a hot smoke that eventually passed and left me shaken but clear, and I thought then I might be done with wanting, or it might be done with me, until you arrived. Are you sure there is nothing else, the priest asked me once in frustration, and I wish I could have said yes, I wish I could have done so much more when there was more to be done, I wish I had been able to tell him *I have sinned and sinned and sinned and will do it again, gladly, until there is no redemption left.*

To give my confessions nobility, now I think of myself as biographer, archivist, witness, doing the important work. Who else will remember? Who else will make it good, make it beautiful, make sense of it all? There were never any marks left. What took place between the two of you, what took place between the three of us, left no proof. Maybe just a scratch where the bed frame moved against the floor, a smudge of dirt where it scraped the wallpaper, an earring rolled under the dresser, dents in the table where the tip of a knife sunk in. I have to remember and recount, even if you are the only one who will listen now.

After that day in the shop I was sure she had decided against a friendship with me. I felt embarrassed, thinking about how I had eaten the apple with her lipstick on it, like I was a young girl swooning. But a few days later I opened the bakery to find a note pushed under the door, white paper with the dusty footprint of my husband on it, so I supposed he hadn't read it. In compact, jagged handwriting she invited me to lunch on Friday. Only me. I was glad my husband hadn't seen it, glad for once of his obliviousness. Later that day when it was quiet I switched our sign from *Open* to *Closed*, ran down the road and asked Josette to watch the shop for me for a couple of hours on Friday afternoon—I had to run some errands, I would pay her. It felt bracing to lie.

When Friday came, I found myself once more in their house, sitting at the large dark table that had been covered in flowers, now unadorned except for three creamy linen placemats. Violet and the ambassador were both there, which I had not expected. She had opened all the curtains but the room did not get much light. There was a pot-au-feu, too dry, carrots, potatoes, none of it memorable. I ate every bite.

Mainly they spoke together in a bickering, easy tone. Their talk felt like warm water washing up against me. Sometimes they addressed a question to me directly, perfunctorily—asking what happened in town in the summer, how was my husband, did I miss the city. I told them my husband was the same as ever, and that I never thought of the city these days. I told them that very little ever happened. They must have thought me quite stupid, and perhaps it suited me to be thought of that way.

I'd like to have a drink with him, the ambassador said. I've been enjoying your local hospitality with a few of the other men. They're very welcoming. Speaking of drinks, come and help me find the next bottle of wine. Guests must choose.

He led me down the stairs to the cellar, where it was cool. It occurred to me that he could easily turn and press me up against the damp stone wall, while he unbuckled his expensive belt, pulled up my skirt, and no one would ever know. He was close enough to touch, I could put out my hand and lay it upon him, and the reality of him took my breath away. I hovered my palm over the shorn black stubble on the back of his neck as he stooped, studying the rack of wine, but I did not touch.

Sometimes I see you in the bakery, he told me, not looking at me, still examining the wine. My hand snatched back. You always look very serene. It's quite beautiful to see. He turned to me suddenly, holding a bottle in each hand. This one? he asked, thrusting a long green bottle towards me. Or this? he said, raising one of a darker glass. Choose carefully, he said. Don't rush it. He passed me the first bottle, cold in my hands, and I pretended to read the label. He passed me the other bottle of wine. I didn't recognize them, unwilling to admit I had never drunk either one nor even heard of the regions which produced them, and I was stricken by the choice I had to make, with his gleaming eyes watching me, mouth red under his beard. I closed my eyes and held up the second bottle. He took it from me.

Wrong, he said, putting it back, his tone amused rather than disappointed.

He followed me up the stairs as I climbed slowly towards the square of light, imagining him putting his hand on the small of my back, or catching my ankle to drag me down. I waited in the kitchen as he found fresh glasses for the wine.

You go ahead, he said. I'll only be a moment.

He smiled as I left the room and when I glanced over my shoulder he was bent over the glasses on the table, turned away from me.

In the dining room, Violet was gazing out of the window, ignoring me, and only looked up when the ambassador placed the glasses on the table.

Thank you. I have a powerful thirst today, she said, taking one of them, but before she could drink from it he snatched it back. That's Elodie's, he said. This is yours. He pushed forward an identical-looking glass.

Oh, sorry, she said, accepting the one he offered. How rude of me. She drained half of it in one go. There are dogs running around outside, she added, standing up and moving to the window. We joined her to see three strays gambolling. As we watched, two men approached them with a large net, each holding one side. The dogs danced out of reach. We heard one of the men curse, then spit on the ground.

Will they bite them? Violet asked.

No, I said, this happens all the time.

Though this wasn't strictly true, it was happening more and more as our abundance increased, as the bad times became more like a distant dream.

They should have people on horseback with brass instruments and drums to scare them away instead, Violet said. Think about how much better that would be.

As we watched, the net landed over two of the dogs and they were tangled in it, raising their foam-flecked jaws up. The third dog ran off as the men pulled their catch to the ground.

What will they do with them now? Violet asked.

They'll take them out into the fields, the ambassador told her. They'll release them into the countryside where they can enjoy hunting rabbits and swimming in the rivers. They'll eat grapes off the vine and get drunk together, they'll have the time of their lives.

I like that, she said. Let's get a dog.

Whatever you want, he said. You know you can have whatever you want.

She smiled at that, started listing things on her fingers. A boat. A pair of diamond earrings. A baby. A black cat. He poured us both more wine.

Later he went off to go and see someone. He always has to go and see someone, Violet told me, as we waved him off at the door, like the house belonged to the two of us. But stay a while. Stay a while, she repeated, with a tremor in her voice. So I stayed—what else could I do?

We're going out later. Help me choose an outfit, she said. She picked up the bottle of wine and led me up the stairs, through the door I had waited outside on the night of the party. It was like step-ping into a dream. In the daytime I could see that the walls were papered in deep green with thin stripes of pale yellow, peeling in the very corners but hardly enough to notice. The furniture was dark wood, traditional, like in the rest of the house.

It's quite old-fashioned. Not what I would have chosen myself, she commented, seeing me take it all in.

Here, I thought, focusing on the tall deep bed. Here is where he knelt before her and spoke about my husband, but not about me. Here is the bed where it all takes place. Here is the coverlet on which he lays her down.

She opened the door of the cupboard and brought out an armful of dresses, some of which I recognized from the lavoir, tossed them carelessly on the bed, then sat on the floor and refilled her glass. Come here, she said, patting the rug. The windows were all open in this room, a sound like the beating of wings, a sky milked over and cooler, heavy, like pudding. I was quite drunk. There was a bruise like a smudge of dirt on her wrist. I pointed at it, touched it, made brave.

Does he beat you? I asked.

Her eyes were closed. Her fingers unfurled, clenched in a fist, relaxed again. I took one hand in mine and touched each pad of her fingers like I was playing an instrument. She laughed unexpectedly, with her mouth wide open. I was in love with her and repulsed by her, like this, so open. I could see her stockings where her dress had ridden up, I could see the gaps in her teeth.

No, he doesn't touch me, she said to me, opening her eyes. There's nothing like that.

You seem very close, I said. Like newlyweds. I'm curious about you.

She sat up, appraised me with something that wasn't quite surprise, as I held my breath, wondering if I had gone too far. She crossed her legs.

You want to know about us? she said. All right then, I'll tell you something. I'll tell you how we really met. It's my favourite story. But only if you don't tell anyone.

She described spilled sugar clouding the surface of a table. Outside, sheets of water. A shining black taxi like a beetle screaming down the street. (I pictured orange light flaming up behind the bar, a tank of water holding two enormous, dirty silver fish. He came along the road in a long black coat, appeared from the shadows. Come in, she thought. Come in. So he did. He walked over to her table. He put money down on it for the coffee, took her wrist. Let's go, he said. She could tell the woman behind the counter was watching, polishing and repolishing the same glass with a red cloth, but she didn't care.)

He found me, she told me, speaking low and flat, as if she were hypnotized. I will never know how he found me, I can't even remember what I was doing earlier that day, but I was in the café counting out my coins, I had enough left for one more coffee. It was so cold and I didn't want to leave. It was raining so hard. He came in and he put the money down himself as if he was making a bet, and then he took my hand, and that moment was the split in my life, between before and after, as if he opened a door into a different world. I took him to my room, she continued. My little room where I lived alone, and I let him undress me before I knew his name. When I was naked before him, I was filled with a great sense of calm. I had been waiting for that certainty my whole life, she told me.

Tell me something else, I said. I was ravenous for details.

She gazed up at the ceiling. All right, she said. He likes me to do things for him. He likes me to wear red lipstick.

Her voice lulled me. (I pictured her going to the mirror with lipstick in hand, him following, watching the movement as she deftly painted her mouth, the clarity cutting through everything, the sorrowful late-afternoon gloom reducing everything to that slash of colour as he unbuttoned his trousers, as she moved to her knees.)

He puts his hand to my head, she told me.

(I pictured her in her light sundresses with no girdle or brassiere beneath, walking around the house she barely kept, knowing so little held her away from nakedness.)

Is it ever like that for you? she asked, but she wasn't really asking. She smiled at me when I answered, Sometimes. She knew it was a lie. (I pictured his hands in her hair, the bones of the knuckles moving under the skin as he gripped tighter, pulling strands of her hair loose, and she told me she would find them in her silver hairbrush afterwards, in front of the mirror before bed, a hundred smooth strokes for luck.)

She was trying on her jewellery by this point, pillaging the box, spreading the glittering gems out on the floor. I put her hand, covered in rings, into my palm. I found the heavy diamond necklace she had been wearing on the night of the party. Let's try it on you, she said, clipping it around my throat as we stood in front of the mirror. Her hands were cool. She watched me in the glass. Behind us the room seemed hazed. She stroked my neck, touched a fingernail to my pulse. At last she removed the necklace and laid it on the dresser in front of us. And this is a moment where I waver each time, the memory of a garish blue bead mixed in with the other trinkets in her jewellery box—sometimes I see it and sometimes I don't. She was still watching me.

We turned to survey the dresses on the bed. Which one? she asked me.

I pointed to the primrose-yellow one I had seen at the lavoir.

Good choice, she said. Undo me?

She turned around and I hesitated for a moment, but she waited and said nothing more, so I stepped forward and unbuttoned her apple-green dress, slipped it off her shoulders so it fell to the floor. She stepped out of it and left it there, pulled the other over her head, dark nipples visible through her gauzy brassiere, ribs arching against her skin with the movement of her arms.

And again, she said, standing still and lifting up her hair, waiting for me to button her up.

She walked away as soon as I finished, disappearing lightly through a door which I assumed led into a bathroom. Without her in the room, I felt once again the strangeness of being there, an interloper. I ran my hands over the objects on her dressing table: silver-backed hairbrush, powder compact inlaid with mother-of-pearl. I lifted her perfume bottle to my nose and sniffed, the surprisingly masculine notes of tobacco, musk, then something sweet underneath. A lipstick like a gold bullet went into my pocket so easily that I forgot I had taken it until later, when I felt the small weight in my dress. Red, like the one in the story she had told me, though I didn't know it then. She returned to the room and, smilingly, drew me out. Downstairs someone had pulled the petals from a vase of flowers in the hall and arranged them around the base, very neatly, not the way they would naturally drop. My hands moved to them, gathered them almost automatically. Violet watched me collect them into a little pile, but said nothing.

When I got home there was a box of the sweets I liked best waiting for me on the kitchen table: dark chocolates with fondant centres, wrapped in red foil. Are these for me? I called to my husband, pleased. Are what? he called back. I put one in my mouth, ignoring his joke. It might be an invitation, I thought hopefully, and it was true that when I undressed that night my husband, who usually looked away, kept his eyes on me. They didn't close or slide past me, they showed no indication of disgust or any other emotion. They rested steadily on me, as he sat up in our bed, as if I were made of marble, or salt, and slowly I felt my hope diminish. Hello? I said, waving my hand in front of his face, and he blinked. Were you asleep? Made bold, I kissed him on the mouth, briefly. His lips tasted like sugar, but he didn't react.

I drew my white cotton nightdress down over my skin and laid myself in bed next to him. What would Violet do? She would run her hand all the way down his chest, she wouldn't take no for an answer, but who would turn her down anyway? There was a queasiness in the progression of these thoughts, the inevitable comparisons between me and her, but I couldn't stop myself moving against my hand, turning over to bury my face into the pillow, as soon as my husband's breathing slowed into sleep. I couldn't tell if what excited me was the image of Violet and my husband specifically, or just the idea that he might still be capable of being seduced by someone, that desire might still live in him somewhere.

Dear Violet,

You kept a bad home, but I liked that about you. I liked the way you let things fall around you and then looked blankly up as if you were surprised by how the situation had degenerated, by the constant and invisible work you were unwilling to do. You were always drinking from days-old glasses of stagnant water. The fabric of the tablecloths and curtains pilled and stained, while insects flung themselves, dying, against the glass of the windows.

You won't be there any more, but I still imagine you walking through those same rooms, lifting your hair, letting it fall. Now I know that your time there quickly became a series of games. Your body was a barometer, alive to what happened inside that house, house of dark corners and floorboards on which you would sometimes find yourself sitting, aimless, looking for signs in the knots of the wood.

Sometimes I step back and try to examine the force of my fascination with you, what drew me up those stairs and into the slice of light where it hit the floorboards. I've always been a good learner, teaching myself things ever since I was a girl. I've had to find it all out myself, I read a lot of books, even though I was Elodie from the country, Elodie serene and bovine, plodding along, thrusting loaves in people's faces. Red cheeks, a spiral of light hair sticking to my forehead, flour on my skirt, strangely ageless, past thirty, not yet forty, unselfconscious, irreproachable. Sometimes I think of you as an ant I could burn under a magnifying glass, if I just look closely enough.

I've decided a few things, I have some theories, if you'd care to respond. I think you were horrified at the idea that he was enough for you, that it was what you needed all along. That a good man was the solution to whatever plagued you, so your mother was right, and the nuns and the matrons, the procession of humourless bitches traipsing through your life with all that dry advice and no magic. What would they have thought about your days in the city, so different from mine in the same city, where you played at counting out your coins, did odd jobs and painted strange things, borrowed money from friends, posed nude for strangers, lay on unfamiliar beds? What would they think about the ambassador, fitting his hands around your whole waist, around your throat?

You told me once that it was like you had woken up in your marriage and in this town one day, sleepwalked into it. I know that feeling now, coming to consciousness as if after an accident. Desire can do that to you. It's pathetic. You told me yourself it was pathetic, and I couldn't disagree. But then here I am, still picking at your veneer, veering even now between giddiness and contempt. I can't stop chewing it over. *What have I done?* you asked me sometimes, never *what has been done to me?*

A few days later Violet came into the bakery unexpectedly in the middle of the day. She seemed agitated, not quite herself, hands twisting and untwisting.

Something to eat? I asked her, and to my surprise she said yes.

Give me some bread, then, she said, standing before me. Two spots of pink on her cheeks. Her eyes were red like she had been crying. I cut her a slice and placed it on the counter, but she stared, made no move to eat it. Then she looked outside at the street.

What's the matter? I asked her.

She looked back to me. I remember the precise choreography of her movements, the raising of a hand a few centimetres, the shift of her face away. Will anyone come in? she asked.

I walked over to the door and turned the sign around. No, I said. Nobody can come in.

Another tilt of her face, then, towards the floor. She sighed. I just don't know, she said. Sometimes I feel so mixed up. On her wrist I noticed more bruising, darker than before but still not much, still faint enough that you might call it a trick of the light.

Marriage is just difficult, isn't it? she said then, meeting my gaze for the first time since she had come in. To love someone else forever and bend them to your will, or bend to theirs. How do you decide who does which? Oh, I don't even know what I'm saying, she said. I'm lonely today I suppose. You've been married longer than me, you probably think I'm talking nonsense.

I remember being so happy in that moment. I remember leaning towards her protectively, though I had little wisdom to impart. My body formed a barrier between her and the world, my solid comforting body, my hands reaching out to her hands.

Is everything all right? I asked her, and the second I said it, it felt preposterous.

Her hands clutched at mine as she looked to the floor. Oh, where to begin, she said, half laughing.

She reached for the bread then and took a bite, and then another, chewed it slowly. It's good, she said, her eyes wet. Her throat remained still.

I don't believe she swallowed it, knowing now that it was all a performance for me, but *performance* still implies a sort of care, a little theatre of desire, so I couldn't be angry about it, even much later, thinking about her wadding the wet bread in her cheek like an animal, thinking about her spitting it out into the road once she was gone.

Dear Violet,

Yesterday I took the train to a city an hour away, on a research mission. At the cinema they were showing a shrill romance. The bored woman in the kiosk pushed my ticket under the window, and in the glass I caught my own reflection, my new hair, and I really could have been you. I thought fondly of the version of you who no doubt went to cinemas alone in the middle of the day too. Your old life and my new one don't seem so far apart now—two indolent, unsupervised women drifting through the afternoons. As I walked through the dark corridors towards the screen, I could almost feel your breath on the back of my neck. When I entered there was only one other person in the red velvet seats, a man, sitting near the back. I didn't look at him.

The film started and I concentrated on it, on the smooth plane of the heroine's cheeks, the orb of a tear resting underneath her left eye. She and the hero must be together, I saw, but in order for that to happen somebody else had to die. They had a plan in motion, all the pieces in place. Their bodies embraced, artificial but graceful. Out of the side of my eye I sensed the man moving a few seats down, closer to me. He made a show of settling into the new seat, stretching out his long legs, but then after a few minutes he moved again.

Your breath was on my neck again. *Get on your knees, Elodie, unbutton his trousers, spit in his face*, you would have told me, had you been there. *These things are possible for you now, these things are owed to you*. Trance-like, I watched the screen cut to a dark street sheeted with water and a man walking along it in a black coat. The hero had a way of putting his hand on his lover's flank that suggested digging his fingers into her ribcage, as he nuzzled against her neck. I decided these were all details worth filing away, and the interiors too, lavish monochrome. I would go home and re-create all this in my imagination later, agonize over each detail until it was perfect, but before that there was the pleasure of taking it in for the first time, opening my eyes as wide as they would go. The man was right next to me by that point, but he made no move to touch me. We both looked straight ahead.

It's terrible, isn't it, he said, still looking ahead. I've seen it every day this week.

Why?

Well, it's the only thing on, and besides, one day I might come and find it different. There might be something I missed.

He raised his hand to the screen. Now she sighs, and then the kiss, he said—and he was right, the actors followed his words as if directed. I know the formula for all of these films, it's always the same, he explained. There's a comfort in that, don't you think? His voice was low, flat, like a hypnotist's.

Perhaps you should read a book instead, I told him. If you're so bored by all of this.

The trap was laid on screen. The lover would kill his wife, or maybe the other woman, it was not clear. She was tied up in a chair—I made a note of it, how the rope bit into the skin at her ankles and wrists, you never know what might come in useful. We looked straight ahead.

I don't want a book, I don't want the trouble of it, he said. I don't want to get involved, I just want to watch what's going on. I know what's going to happen and then it happens, and I can go outside and feel good about it, I can leave it in the room. A book hangs around, but an image is just a moment.

I don't believe that at all, I said.

Believe what you want, he told me. It's up to you.

When the film ended the room was cast into darkness. I stood up first and walked away along the rows of seats. He followed me, his breathing quick. He's a pervert, I thought to myself with a certain comfort. He's a murderer and he's in love with me. The corridor was deserted, glowing softly red at the end as though I were walking along a vein. When I slowed my steps he slowed his too, I thought I sensed his arm reaching out to me, hand resting over the nape of my neck, moving down to the small of my back. Then his voice, low in my ear. Tell me your telephone number, he said, and so I stopped, I stood still and recited the number of my landlady out loud without turning to him. Say it again, he said, and I recited it once more, slowly, with feeling. Don't move, he told me. He overtook me and walked rapidly into the fading light. Don't move, I told myself. I remained standing there, as still as possible, until two laughing women started walking down the corridor, their laughter pausing as they noticed me, as they tried to understand what I was doing there.

The train took me home in a rush and all the lights we passed shone cleanly in the rain. Safely back in my room, my blood coursing, I was hungry for images. Reaching under the bed I took out the magazines which come in the post, ordered out of curiosity or necessity, and always with shame. After spreading them on the floor in front of me and turning on all the lights, I studied the photographs like maps. Women with their breasts in their hands and their legs open. On a chair with their legs crossed or lying on the ground, viewed sideways, garters and black stockings, red lipstick, girdle then no girdle, a progression of sorts. Smudges of hair under the arms, between the legs, glimpsed only, bending over something, looking behind, it wasn't enough, it's never remotely enough. But I am afraid of wearing out my memories like old clothes tried on too many times, Violet, and the fear of my memories losing their power is always battling with the fear of the totality of memory making my life unbearable, so I have to mend and refigure with what's available, I have to do it while I still can. And so I looked at the images and decided what could be used and what could be discarded, what would do for patching up the scenes you've left behind, what could feel real, what you would have done, what could have been done to me.

I knew the others in the town watched her too, maybe not as closely, but enough to be useful. The grocer's wife came into the shop one day with crystallized fruit and information. Here you go, she said, putting the little box of sweets, tied with a gold ribbon, down on the counter. I was touched. She has me order these in, she explained. I've been dying to try them myself.

What else does she order? I asked. Made sure to be scornful, made sure to pick a fresh loaf for her and wrap it up and slide it across the counter in a way that made it clear there was no charge. Gold afternoon light spilled everywhere, warmed the whitewashed stone of the walls. The red floor tiles needed sweeping. The grocer's wife seemed tired and I felt strangely maternal towards her suddenly, this younger woman with her easy prettiness.

She leaned in. She orders olives in tins, truffles, big bars of chocolate, she told me. We send away for it. Money is no object. Cocoa powder and meat pastes and sweets. Whatever she wants.

And how does she seem to you? I asked her. Do you think she's settling in? (The marks under her skin, the blue under her eyes; she sat in bed and devoured chocolate almost without chewing on it, her fingers and palms sticky, teeth filmed.) I unwrapped the paper around the crystallized fruits and chose a segment of orange dense with sugar, offered the box to the grocer's wife. She took a grape.

She's cold, isn't she? she said. Really quite rude, in fact. Something else too, I can't place it. She shuddered theatrically. I don't know what he sees in her. But him!

She waved away the box when I offered it a second time. Actually, I'm quite nauseous, she told me, shyly.

Oh! I said. I gave her more bread, gave her as much as she could carry, because after all I was very happy then, and how good it felt to live in a place where happiness was possible, for me and for all those around me.

Scrap after scrap of information to sustain me. (Violet picked apart a candied raspberry, her lipstick worn off in the middle. A hole in her stocking that she curled her toe around to hide, an imperfection that made my heart sing.) I closed the shop and stepped outside into the late sunshine, moving through the crowd of the market with a basket on my arm, smoothly, dreamily, like somebody in love. The other women moved around me, nodded, kicked at the stray cats. It smelled unseasonably hot and dry, the clouds all burned away. Bunches of flowers were laid out on the tables and propped in buckets beside them. The people pressed against each other as they picked up potatoes, inspected them for rotten parts. Red tomatoes splitting at the seams in wooden crates, the wasps crawling over and into them, the sellers shouting and the women shouting back, *lower*, haggling prices. (Meanwhile Violet, pale, lying with her arms thrown out in the big country bed. Downstairs the ambassador making her coffee. His step on the stairs; she closed her eyes. He sat her up, gave her the cup, she drank deep.)

My husband was standing at the sink when I came in. (*Do you want to fuck him?* the ambassador asked, he never stops asking, one day she will say yes.) I cut new strawberries lengthwise on a plate, into little hearts. When he turned around I put one in my mouth, slowly, let him see my tongue and lips. Did he wince? I tried another. Eat one, I said, putting it to his mouth. He closed his own lips, closed his eyes. I pressed harder, until the red flesh mashed against them. My happiness dissipated. His eyes opened and he was blank as a pebble, mouth stained. I went upstairs to try something new. The lipstick I had stolen from Violet lay in a drawer next to the oyster shells from the party, and with great care I applied it, but before I had finished I heard the door slam. When I went back downstairs, he was gone, and Violet was sitting on a chair. If she noticed the lipstick, she didn't say anything.

Hello, she said. I hope you don't mind me dropping by. Your husband let me in. He seemed in a rush.

She didn't ask me what had happened. Sit down, she said, even though it was my house not hers, and I obeyed her. She leaned forward and said, Do you want to see something secret?

I forgot the humiliation of the strawberries. I nodded.

Together we walked east, along the main road, heading out of town. Picturesque, she commented as we passed the river. She was right, it was beautiful, with the water softly gleaming and the stone buildings beside it regal, only slightly worn.

It's like living in a painting, she said. Maybe somebody somewhere is watching us. We're hanging on somebody's wall. My father had a painting when I was growing up, of a shepherdess in a meadow, and every night I used to say a prayer to swap places with her. I would lie there in the bed with my arms crossed over my body, willing myself to wake up in the lush meadow with nothing to do but sit there with a lamb in my arms. Her hair was in long braids, and the colours were all cool blues and greens. How nice it would have been to sit behind glass watching the others walking around the house, to feel the soft wool under my hands all day, don't you think?

We were out of the town by then. We walked across the dry fields, climbed over gates with our skirts pulled high. The wavering heat summoned far-off horizons, incantatory shapes in the clouds. Another gate, another field, her helping me down, taking my hand in hers briefly. Dry yellow grass.

They hated me, my parents, she said, quite cheerfully. They wished I had never been born. My mother said I was born with a toad in my heart. She kicked easily at a clod of dirt. I like to walk here, she said. It's so flat and wide. Like being in a desert. Sometimes I'd like the whole world to recede altogether. She pointed to something in the distance. Large shapes, soft and strange, still on the ground. Look, she said.

We drew closer. The smell of rot grew stronger as we approached, and I held my breath. The air moved and droned with flies, dipping and then resting on the shapes, which I saw now were motionless horses. There were no visible wounds, no froth around the mouths, just stillness. They upset me deeply—the heaviness of them, the positioning almost graceful, these bodies which seemed like they could rise at any time and sprint through the landscape. We counted eight of them, lined up neatly. We walked around them in a circle, like a spell.

We must tell the police, I said, as she knelt down next to one, hovered her hand over the glossy reddish-brown of its coat. She batted away the flies from its open eye.

But what if we don't, she said. What if we just leave them as they are? After all, it's nothing to do with us. I just wanted to show them to you, I wanted to be sure they were real.

And so we went back, taking a slightly different route that time, one that took us by the lake where the children screamed in the water, the trees bordering it, and she was right, I realized as I watched green leaf-light shimmer across her face—nobody had to know, or at least not from us. I've forgotten them already, haven't you? she said, and when she said it like that, I knew I almost had.

We sat under a tree together, her bright, me still nauseated, and she began talking about her childhood. She told me about the visions that came to her like waking dreams, the flowers in the garden possessed with faces that stared at the sun and then stared at her, malevolent. The slipperiness in the drape of the curtains. She had realized that the barrier between one world and the next was not really a barrier at all, at best a sheet of silk, able to flicker and let the light through.

She was sent away for her schooling, somewhere high and remote. When she was fifteen she wrote long letters in cursive script to a girl outside of the boarding school walls who she had met once. *We had ice cream for dessert when we went into town. I had pistachio and vanilla. My father sent me a bracelet of real gold for my birthday. There is a pink rabbit that lives under my bed, I have named him Victor. The girl next to me broke her arm falling off horse-riding, she screamed for an hour.* Sometimes the eyes of her reflection wouldn't meet her own in the mirror. The letters were intercepted eventually, the girl had become disturbed at their content and frequency. The answers to everything unrolled like a carpet. *I'm listening,* she told the world outside her window, bathed in cool, fine air, a sheen of snow. *I'm listening.* And I listened too. It was the most beautiful story I had ever heard, more intimate than anything she could have told me about sex. It did make me feel better. Her eyes were fixed on the leaves of the trees above us.

I've never spoken to anyone about these things, she said. I spent some time in hospital too, just a few months, before the war. The strange ideas came back, you see. And it was horrible, Elodie, but nice too, not to have to think about anything. I was wrapped in wool because I was breakable. It was like being in the painting after all. They gave me so much medicine that my mind separated from my body, like I could carry my head around under my arm and just put it down if I ever needed a break. I put it down quite a lot—at first, anyway. But I got better, just in time, because I wouldn't have liked to be mad through those years, would you?

No, I said.

Though maybe it wasn't so bad here, she said.

It was quite bad here, I said, thinking of the sky on fire, nights in the bakery cellar pressed close to the others. It was bad everywhere.

The word *love* wasn't broached, but it throbbed under every syllable. By the time she had stopped telling me things, the nausea was gone.

The next day in the bakery everybody was excited and fearful and wanted to talk about the horses. Their bellies were split wide open, said Mme G, she who loved the gruesome and arcane, in her usual black dress. She talked with an animation I hadn't seen in years.

Their insides all over the ground, she added, almost smacking her lips. Something had been feeding on them. A wolf, maybe, or a dog, but what animal could tear the stomach so neatly? Something supernatural, she told me. Some kind of devil skulking about, something soul-sucking and sharp-toothed. She told me that she knew I must think her a stupid old woman, but she'd scattered a handful of grass seeds to the wind, noticed the portents in the stars. One day you'll know those things too, she said, when you're like me, it'll be here before you know it. You'll be old and the others will be old and you'll still be at the lavoir every week, and evil will come all the time, evil woven into the world inescapably, under the surface, waiting for its moment, that's how it goes.

Mme A shared, nervously, that the hooves had been cut off. And the blood, I was told by the grocer's wife, who had heard it from her husband. The blood had been drained. But when I asked for proof, everybody was evasive. I asked them again and again, knowing they were wrong in every detail, and I felt a dark joy in being the one who knew. Even when I went home and that night my husband turned away from me like he had done on hundreds of nights before, I still had that, I still knew that she and I had been the only ones to see. And I was so glad, then, that we had left the bodies quiet in the heat, as if we had never been there.

Dear Violet,

The police came back today. Looser, more brisk this time. There's
something about this case they can't leave alone. I imagine them
dreaming of it each night, lurid visions still puzzling them at
breakfast. Even their unremarkable morning baguettes, broken
hungrily, might seem strange. They sat in my room with their hats
in their hands as I made them coffee, again.

We almost didn't recognize you, the kinder one said.

A disguise? the crueller one added.

In return for platitudes and evasion, they gave me the latest
updates. Twelve people still in the asylum. No further deaths. I
reminded them of my own husband, lying in the graveyard where
his parents and their parents before them lie, and they rewarded
me with some fleeting compassion. The kinder one slopped coffee
in his saucer, hands shaking. I saw the other one notice, frown.
Yes, I still see things. Still watch forensically, just in case.

Are you sure you haven't remembered anything? they asked me.

I lost my mind, I told them. I was as insensible as the rest.

But you can't recall anything new, anything at all? the cruel one pressed.

No, I told him. I didn't tell him that sometimes I wake up and once more am the creature I was on that day, with my bloody fingernails, and my limbs unrecognizable. Or that waves of colour still come to me, bearing down like water, or that every so often there are shapes in the corners of my eyes, a swooping, like a great bat. I want no doctor to rid me of them, to press a thermometer against my tongue or examine my eyes. They make me think of the visions that came to you too, and though I know mine were chemically triggered—cheating, I guess, I wasn't tuned into the universe's frequencies in the way you are—still, when I see those things it feels like I might be seeing the world the way you do.

I think about the tracking of poisons or dyes in the body, Violet, how the colour blooms through the veins, how the pathways all light up. I try to understand what I was to you but it's all tangled up. How trite it was, in the end, you playing at transcendence like it would save you from the little domesticities of your lot, the things you felt beneath you, the things that were only for women like me. Water and soap and flour, sweat-marked linen and butter and lye and buttons and thread—how could they possibly compete with the life you had imagined for yourself, up there in the mountains?

We are so often wrong about those we love, slowly debasing ourselves, so gradually we barely notice we're doing it. The intimacy of our afternoons blurred the truth for both of us, don't you agree? Perhaps you really were raised in the woods, or found buried in a patch of earth like a potato, or discovered swimming in a teardrop of dew, your arms batting wide. Perhaps I really did sit inside your bedroom, watchful, observing you and the ambassador as your bodies made the same old recursive movements, each one predictable, each one a stunning invention never before thought of. I picture you sometimes as a set of Russian dolls, each layer revealing nothing except a tiny, weaker version of yourself, at the end only hollowness. You made yourself a character in your own story, at least as much as I made you a character in mine. Now it's impossible to know what I was told and what I created. You become less than, more than, yourself. You take up the very air and I can hardly breathe, but I have faith that it will exhaust itself one day, Violet, that one day I will be done with all of this.

I have been drawing today—another way of copying you, I know, but I can't resist reaching out to you, clumsy marks on the paper like a record of my attempts to look and see. And there's a satisfaction in being the one to make the images now, though I know you'd laugh at them. I drew the items in my collection, arranged on the small pine table in my room. No rain today, good light, the sweep of deserted sand. An oyster shell, the lustre worn off with time. One stocking, nude, well preserved. A dark red lipstick used down to the nub, still reverently painted on my mouth at times, but rationed, now, positioned with the lid off. A length of ribboning black silk against which they all lay. Divested of their votive power, they didn't really cohere as a still life. Yet I persevered, repositioning them again and again as if that might be the key to the composition working, seeking some arrangement where it all made sense.

I imagined your hand holding my pencil. It was no good but I finished it anyway, the humiliation of my inability was partly the point, it's just busywork to pass the time. Drinking as I drew, I spilled some wine, scrubbing at the red ring left on the table by the bottle. With one hand I marked the wine level, checked my consumption. There is a sweet spot. Two glasses in, the objects became unnerving and so I pulled on my coat and walked down the street to the café with the green tiles shining on the wall. The waiter smiled, discreetly wiping my table and bringing me a glass of wine unbidden. Sometimes the process of being in the world feels easy, sometimes it does not. There was a time when I used to sit in the cold storeroom of a different café, before I met my husband and my life began or ended, depending on how you look at it—a time when I sat in the back of the café on my breaks, reading novels and eating apples. Since I left the bakery I have not been able to read a novel, it seems to be one of the lingering side effects, and even biting into a crisp piece of fruit can feel overwhelming, the crunching of it inside my jaw like it's the skull of a smaller animal.

The waiter came over again with the newspaper, already out of date. I took in every fact: a corrupt politician taking a bribe, the child mauled by a dog fifty kilometres away, a war being fought even further away than that, the reassurance of all the tragedies in the world ready to take the place of ours, moving us gently downstream. Two more glasses then, and only a piece of bread for sustenance, I rose from my table and walked out into the street, one foot stepping gracefully into a square of light, then back to darkness. It's risky to let myself become so drunk, it lets in that strange and searching light, the possibilities of what I remember opening up in a way I know could destroy me, and yet increasingly I want to look towards it, that light, to see the shape of what has happened and what could have happened up ahead of me on the road, just out of reach. My feet moved along the promenade and my hand was on the cold iron rail and I knew the streak of water to the right was the sea, which I knew could not freeze, and yet the dead could still walk towards me on its surface, moving slow and salted, coming to take me with them. I forced myself not to run, though the shapes pressed ever closer to me.

Now I am safely back in my room, though it never truly feels safe from what I know is waiting for me. To have you with me would be a comfort, Violet, compared to all of this. I closed my eyes when I came in as if to conjure the two of you up—pictured you standing quiet by the table, still as mannequins, waiting to direct or be directed—but when I opened my eyes you were not there.

There are humiliations a person might never recover from, Violet, but you wouldn't know that. When I am with somebody else, I try to exist in my own body, in my own mind. I ask the men I bring back here to do all the things I wanted your husband to do to me, and then I ask them to say the things I wished your husband had said, to give me the experience I deserve. It's within reach, I know it—the same way I know when I reposition the oyster shell by half a centimetre, when I carefully wind the lipstick out from its case. The choreography is delicate, but I know every step of it now, and there's no shame for me in the asking for it, though I can see it in the eyes of the men, the surprise and the contempt. It can't be done alone, it needs another. Alone, I content myself with remembering the two of you, expansive and a little disgusted too. Without the constraints of my own body, everything can take place. I can harm you, ruin you, I can watch the blood coursing from your mouth. Does it help? you may ask. Yes—it helps a little.

After all, it seems that the small details are the ones that last. Your lipstick worn off in the middle, the dirty soles of your feet. The pale mark left on his wrist by the strap of his watch, the light film of sweat on his forehead and the rest of him pristine. I should have done more, when there was more to be done. Should have stored more things away, should have understood that my life would become a process of remaking.

Watch me, heating soup on the hotplate. Watch me, watching myself, in the mirror hanging across the room. A flash of colour in the corner of my eye; dreams, sticking to me, a faint weight like your hand, holding me down when I wake. I've been looked at in pity and in fear and I've learned that the only way to really be seen is through desire. To be looked at and found whole. Found alive. Please look at me. I promise you that I am here.

I was so intent on watching her that I barely noticed the summer creeping into the fresh mornings, but all of a sudden it was upon us. It made us all lighter, I think, the promise held inside the new days, each one warmer than the last. Violet took me shopping in the next town over, larger than ours and more prosperous, and I tried on dress after dress, a hand at my waist, fingers pressed hard under my ribcage. She made me twirl around. Dance, she said. Move around, more. You're not an old woman, not yet. And you're not like the others. She said the name of the grocer's wife like it was a bad smell. I can't stand her, she said. She's like a puddle of water, a dirty one. Not worth the trouble it takes to step in it. She fussed with my buttons, stepped back to consider me. There, you see, that's not so bad, she said.

We decided together on two new dresses, more fashionable than any I owned, one sky-blue and one striped, grey on white. I'll buy them for you if you won't get them yourself, she said. Look, you're still young, I can't bear it when you pretend that you're not.

Violet's care absolved me of a lot. She wanted the best for me, even when I didn't want it for myself.

She helped me out of the blue dress and I stood before the mirror in my brassiere and girdle, faded cream cotton, miserable. I sweated like I was sick. Skin spilled out from under the straps. Violet clucked. She took a step forward so we were eye to eye in the mirror. Poor Elodie, she said. And poor Violet, too.

She put her hand on my waist and turned me to face her. She was shorter than me, looking up at me like it was a dare, then she tipped forwards onto her toes and kissed me, roughly but not passionately, like a child trying something out. Our teeth clashed. I stumbled, almost fell over, with the force of her. Her hand moved to the back of my head to pull me in closer, and she sucked my tongue, briefly, into her mouth; I laughed at that, stunned, and she laughed too. My body shook as she put me back in my shapeless blouse, my skirt. Her hands were quick. I felt a cool wash of fear. That wasn't so bad, was it, she said, as if she could sense it, and she placed her smooth hand at the small of my back to correct my posture.

On the way to the cash register she casually scooped up an ice-pale blue dress trimmed with lace, much more beautiful than the ones I was buying, not bothering to try it on. I know what he likes, she said, and he'll like this.

The next Tuesday I watched my own hands rinsing my husband's linen shirts, hands disembodied beneath the surface of the water. Mme G was still washing Violet's clothes. The others gathered around her to inspect what the week had yielded, but I stayed where I was.

Oh, look at the detailing here, the grocer's wife sighed enviously over a white dress. How lovely, how lovely.

A full-skirted navy-blue dress with a sober white collar was swiftly discarded. They wanted froth and fripperies, and I did too, though I feigned not to be listening.

Come over here, called Mme F. Don't pretend you're too good for this. She held up the new dress, the one I had watched Violet buy, cackling. Where does the silly little thing wear all these? she asked me, holding it up to examine the seams. You never tell us anything.

How should I know? I said, but I relented then, joining them around the laundry basket.

We see you going in and out of that place, don't think you haven't been seen, they said, and I remember it as if it were in unison, a chorus. It was true that I was spending more and more time with Violet, leaving Josette to watch the shop, claiming I felt unwell or had urgent errands. I glanced over at my accomplice and she caught my eye, knowingly, before looking away.

What's the house like? Tell us more, Mme G insisted.

But I wouldn't tell them about the dirty plates in the sink, the dust carpeting her floors. My loyalty was unwavering. I was there so much that standards were starting to slip in my own house, another thing I could not admit to the women at the lavoir, though my husband had not noticed the change in our home, or if he had he did not say.

Their hands moved through her dirty clothes with eagerness. Do you ever see him? the grocer's wife asked. Is he there when you go over? What's he like?

I pictured her own husband, older than us and very clean, neat, joyless. I pictured mine, still handsome, silent, the fair hair fading to grey at the sides. Not like the ambassador with his tailored suits, entirely out of place and worn with total comfort, the white flash of his teeth. All the men were falling over themselves to befriend him, especially during those nights of *local hospitality* at the bar, which were becoming quite the routine of late (the landlord unable to believe his luck, polishing all the glasses and ordering in extra barrels of beer, bottles of spirits). There were others who held him in suspicion, but still they found themselves combing their hair the same way he did, greeting the others with a handshake or shoulder-clap in the manner they publicly derided as self-important, taste-less, American. What could I say to the women at the lavoir? He was a threat, he was a visitation, he was a promise of elsewhere.

Put this on, Mme F told Josette, suddenly, handing over the blue dress. You're small enough for it to fit.

Mama, no, she protested, shaking her head. What if somebody sees?

Come on, Josie, she cajoled. Just for a minute. I'd do it myself if I could.

No! she said. I don't want to.

Mme F stepped forward and slapped her daughter's face, then immediately looked down at her own palm as if astonished by what she had done. Josette raised her hand to her cheek.

Quickly, the girl pulled her dress up over her head. We glimpsed her body for a second, still childlike beneath her slip, before she was encased in the stiff blue fabric. We were silent. She spun around, gathered up the skirts in a swooping motion, let them fall. It was too big for her. Well? she said.

The grocer's wife grinned in a way that suddenly seemed wolf-ish. She delved into the clothes basket, reaching for the white dress. When she took off her own we saw her breasts swollen and veined in her brassiere. The dress was tight, too tight.

You'll rip it, warned Mme G as she tried to force it, so she left it hanging, smock-like, strangely. They looked over to me. Try one, Elodie, they said.

I picked the deep pink cotton, stepping into it, not bothering to button it up at the back. There was no mirror in which to see myself, only the still water of the lavoir with the remnants of the suds like a swirl of cream.

What about you, we goaded each other then, *What about you*, until even the oldest matrons were wearing something of hers, a blouse or a skirt, and at that point things did start to rip as we danced and moved in her clothes. Her life didn't fit our bodies. Someone was laughing hysterically, and when I felt wetness on my face I realized it was me, but soon everybody else was laughing too.

Josette took off the blue dress first, spooked, as if someone had caught her, and bundled it back into the pile. We came back into ourselves then, the spell broken, and we struggled out of the clothes, tearing them more as we stripped them off, trying not to panic when they bound us tight. They lay on the side of the lavoir, a pile of unravelling seams. We stared at the damage.

What will we do about this? I asked, fretfully.

I bet she won't even notice, said Mme G. She has too many things. Besides, it's only a little loose thread. Let her come and ask us, if it bothers her so much. She looked sideways at me. If she asks anybody, it will be you.

I did not contradict her. We retreated to our proper places round the lavoir, our own piles of washing. As I reached into my basket to retrieve the next soiled shirt, I let fall the pair of Violet's stockings which I had taken, slipping them into my skirts when I gave up the pink dress, while no one was paying attention to anything but themselves.

Even then I was starting to think of myself as her confessor. Both the person seeking absolution and the one providing it can be called the same name. Afternoons of wine and fruit peeled, arranged on a plate, my hands rough and trembling. Maybe there were not so many as it seemed to me, but each one felt endless, languid and boiled in its own syrup. She lay with her eyes closed and my finger would drift to the naked patch of skin underneath her ear, but never touch. My lips made soothing noises, or sometimes I tried not to make any sound at all, so that she would forget I was there, so that she would keep talking, telling me things as if dictating a diary entry.

After that afternoon at the lavoir, I did feel guilty. I was nervous, as if she might somehow sense my betrayal, see it on my face or hear it in my voice. I avoided her for a few days, but it wasn't long before I went back.

Where have you been? she asked, and I smiled and shrugged. It wasn't difficult to distract her from my absence.

Will you tell me about your wedding? I asked, and she smiled then too.

I went into the café next to the church, to use the bathroom before the ceremony, and everybody in there applauded. I don't know why I bothered, because you could barely see my face with the veil. It was old-fashioned, but I liked that. I wanted to pretend I was a virgin, that nothing had ever happened to me. I even believed it, I think.

As she spoke, I saw it. The two old women brought in from the road outside, to be their witnesses, a small child with them. It was two weeks since the night they had met, the scattered sugar on the table, her heart seizing in her chest. She knelt down to the child, who was dressed in lace, shoes shining.

I told her not to be afraid, she said.

I pictured Violet holding her small hand, thinking she was scared of the cold statues, of the priest in his black gown. I pictured the way the child might have looked at the ambassador with a child's animal instinct, the way that dogs swerved around him in the road, the way that horses bucked and failed to obey. Yet he must have walked into the church unharmed, with no thunderous crack or burning sensation across his neck or bleeding from the eyes. He kissed the fragile hands of the old women and kissed Violet's hands again too.

Even in the church he filled the space, she said. His voice was everywhere, echoing. All those stupid words you tell each other. I promised to obey him until I was dead.

I had cried on my own wedding day, first out of gratitude and then out of disappointment. My mother-in-law pulled at my hair under the veil. Everyone in the town was there to see us in the church, celebrating the marriage of a man they had known since he was born, to a woman they had never met. Afterwards there were barrels of beer and a floor on which I was flung around. A wedding wasn't for two people, but for the world. My husband was too drunk to consummate the marriage, throwing up in a bucket beside the bed while his father banged a broom on the ceiling below to tell us to be quiet.

Easier and more enviable to retreat into Violet's account, then. How underneath the chiffon she was already wet. How after the ceremony the ambassador raised the necklace of small intricate diamonds and clipped it around her throat. Love is an abdication, he told her. Will you do whatever I want you to do? The necklace was very tight and the stones were sharp. With pleasure, she told him. He brushed her hair as she sat at the dressing table, one hundred strokes for luck, and she was nothing but nerve, flesh, breath. Have you ever wanted to die? the ambassador asked her, later. She lay very still. Nothing like that, she told him, and then afterwards they drank champagne, sitting by the window wrapped in robes, watching the rain come down.

Dear Violet,

The murderer from the cinema rang my landlady, who knocked on my door and told me to use the telephone in the parlour. She sat back down to knit a shapeless red thing and watched me talk. Can I see you? he asked. The line crackled. I gave him the address of a nearby bar, told him to come the next day. The perversity of having nothing left to lose is growing on me.

In the bar the next day I waited, wearing my own lipstick for a change. The colour doesn't quite work now with my dark hair. Perhaps I'll go to the city and buy new things, I thought into my wine. I could take the train and visit department stores, drink a little vermouth, have a cigarette at a table and watch the crowds moving downstream, all those people with places to go. Perhaps I'll buy your perfume, I still remember the brand. Oh, I bet you're infuriated at that idea—look at me winding you up! It's irresistible. But it was easy to be content there, the wine spreading warm through my veins, the rain soft outside, amber glow of the lamps. You can witness the unthinkable, you can have the unthinkable done to you, and at some indeterminate point in the future you can still be happy, even if just for a fixed moment, a little ball of satisfaction in the chest—isn't that incredible? Even blood washes out, or you can fill your mouth with things that hide the taste of it.

The barman wiped down the surfaces with a blue rag. I tried to see myself as someone else might see me, framed by the window, my head held high. This long piece of flesh is still good, still holds its shape. In certain lights my puckering skin is barely noticeable, you can't tell a lot about me, I think, I hope, can't really tell my age or the size and shape of the ragged wound in my chest. A man came through the door, shook the water from his umbrella, sat opposite me. He tapped me twice on the arm as if waking me up.

All right then, it was ordained from the first time I heard his voice in the dark of the cinema that he would come back to my room. In the stairwell, the light was broken. He walked behind me, below me, put a hand on the back of my thigh. I heard his breathing grow heavy, I slowed my steps. His hand lifted higher, his fingers brushed the edge of my stocking. I looked back and he seemed stricken. In the last months I have reconsidered my body and look, see, it can still hold its power. It's still good, puckering flesh and all. My breath came in bursts. In the room he looked up at the rose of damp on my ceiling, took off his brown raincoat. I put a scarf over the lampshade to dim the light. When he stood by the sink, washing his hands, I could pretend he was your husband, though he was younger, shorter, thinner. I put my hands on his back and I pretended he was the ambassador before I ever saw him moving through the water of that lake—we were strangers meeting in a bar somewhere else with the light flaming behind us, before he got to you. How I would have liked a blindfold for his eyes, a blindfold for my own, just temporarily, just to settle in.

I almost wanted to remain in that moment before anything had happened, relishing the possibilities of what might come next without having to see them through. He turned around, his hands still wet, then his hands on me.

There is a script, I explained before things went any further.

You're the one I wanted all along, he said dutifully once I had worked through it all, running a hand up my leg.

Say it again, I replied. Slower, and drop your voice lower too.

He repeated the line, moving his hand more slowly this time, pausing to trace a small circle with his thumb at my knee. If he was curious, he asked no questions. Images came to me—hands around your throat, Violet, your neck wrung, your body bending like a leaf. My fantasies and reality found a common ground, they found a sort of life, I was touched, I was unbuttoned, kissed on the neck. You're the one I wanted all along, he said again though I hadn't asked him to, an improvisation I could accept, by then I was in an instinctive state, absorbed in the white light of it, I didn't even need you any more. This is what I reach through sex, these days—forgetting you through inhabiting you, something approaching obliteration.

Afterwards he soaped up at the sink, trousers undone. He had done everything I asked of him, and I appreciated that, gratified that the difficult alchemy had been pulled off. Relief, with a well of terror underneath it, because what if it stops working one day, what if I only find out when I'm naked and waiting, what then? He sat on the bed, got dressed. We shared a cigarette. He smoothed down his dark hair, put a hand out to my flank. He kissed me with some melodrama, one hand clutched to my face, and then he left swiftly.

Does it surprise you, Violet, how efficient I can be with my own desire? I am more effective than you gave me credit for. I've done more than you realize, I just couldn't tell you about any of it, not when it seemed so small next to your experiences. My little stabs towards pleasure were clumsy, yes, and not always successful, but sometimes. How pathetic they would seem to you. I never fucked anybody on the bakery counter after all. I never laid a man down by the lake or in the fields where the horses rotted. But on three occasions I told my husband I was visiting my sister in the north, and I took the train alone and I walked around for days in my no-longer-fashionable dress, eyes red-rimmed from the wind. On every windswept corner I willed wonder to arrive but everything I saw reminded me that I was only watching and not experiencing, everything seemed flat and disconnected, until I walked into a bar and slipped my ring into a pocket, and I waited for a man to approach me and then took him back to whatever stale-smelling room I was staying in.

Afternoon light through a smeared window, creased sheets, single beds trimmed like cakes with yellowing valances, water moving syrupy down the plughole of an enamel sink, voices in the hall lilting higher then back to low. The edges of those memories are worn purposefully smooth now, made nice, made good, because that is how you keep on going when there are little betrayals stuck like pins in your stomach, meaningless things that could have been more sordid, perhaps I wanted them to be more sordid, to have my face rubbed in it, perhaps the sordid can be as transformative as the divine if it goes far enough. I'm still working it out. Those men were kind to me, too kind. Did I want someone to spit in my face? Did I want someone to kick me in the side? We're back to that idea of obliteration, Violet. What could ever be enough? Perhaps my desire is always going to turn on me, snap at my hand even when I've fed it, twist into new and unruly shapes. But you see, how could it be your fault, when it started as long ago as that, long before we met? The fault is in me, was in me from the start. These are the things I think about in this little room, where past and present knock up against each other.

Serene Elodie, bovine Elodie, lying face down on a bed, damp and pale as bread soaked in milk, strong limbs used to swimming, now limp, palms facing up, *What will you do to me* I always used to wonder, *What will be done to me.* When I turned over and their faces slid over me, I would catch a slight disgust at my corporeality. My appeal was specific, I was like a mother or a sister, you couldn't pin just anything on me, and it was always possible they would change their mind, get up and walk out. I had no choice but to remain aware of this possibility, there was something conscious or unconscious in their demeanour that would never let me forget it, the provisional quality of their desire. But you, Violet—you have never been denied or walked out on. You will always find a desire reciprocated, no matter how bleak. And in the end, that's just another thing I can't forgive.

That year, our appetite for the midsummer festival had finally returned. In the years preceding, our hearts hadn't really been in it. We tried, we really did, but the bonfires made us flinch, the hot flames and the loud popping of the branches as the sap of the wood boiled and burst. The fires weren't even so high, not like they used to be, because there were fewer of us and less to go around anyway. Mostly we drank, rousing ourselves to dance when we were drunk enough, falling over each other.

In my first years in the town, the festival was a time when I would share some rare intimacy with my husband, as if the heat and the movement awoke something in him. That all stopped during the war, and for a while it seemed like it would never return, but the year before Violet arrived, we had pressed together clumsily in the kitchen when we got home from the festival, smoky skin to smoky skin, both barely able to stand, and he had bent me businesslike over the table where I served our dinner, though he had been too drunk to stay hard for more than a minute or two. Still, it was better than nothing, though I was so drunk myself that sometimes, when I set that table afterwards, I wondered if I had imagined it.

He liked to tell me about jumping over the embers as a young man, about how he had once set his trouser leg on fire. Every year I enjoyed watching his face soften as the familiar words formed in his mouth. The incident with the trousers had left him with a patch of burned skin on his shin, a perfect oval of hairless pink like an egg. He called it his mark from God, though he wasn't usually religious that way, and whether he meant it was a blessing or a curse I never knew. He had run across the field still aflame to plunge his leg into a trough of water. He was covered in hair elsewhere—legs, shoulders, a whole pelt on his chest—and it might have been the hair which had saved him from worse injury, singeing up as it did. Though maybe he hadn't been so hairy then, when he was a young man; I did ask him but he said he couldn't remember, which seemed incredible, because I remembered the litany of my body's features and functions with excruciating detail from the age of twelve onwards, as if a spotlight had suddenly been trained on me. If nothing else, bathing with my many siblings had done that, all of them younger than me, prodding and pointing at my flesh like I was a strange animal in their midst, so that I always seemed covered in fingerprints, whereas he was an only child.

Mark from God because it was lucky the burn didn't go any deeper. Mark from God too because none of the other young men jumping over the embers that year caught fire.

You weren't tempted by the girls jumping over the fire too? I asked him, the same way I did every year. What about Mme A? Or the grocer's wife?

He shook his head. Oh, you know Annette was always too annoying, even back then. And Marie was just a child.

And the others? I asked, trying to provoke him, just a little. I wanted to know about furtive kisses down by the river, knees and backs wet with leaf-smelling mud, or about unlocking the door to the bakery and ferrying girls into the dark when his father was elsewhere, making a shelter behind sacks of flour. He smiled easily, seeming almost bemused.

I chose you, he said.

It was true that no woman had ever pulled me over for a word about my husband, no warning or threat. Nobody had ever shot me a baleful glance at church or complained that I gave her stale loaves, or at least not that I had noticed.

On the day preceding the festival we prepared cherry and strawberry tarts, and special brioche, cut and plaited into complicated shapes. The grocer's wife came by early in the morning with the fruit and stayed to help, nimble fingers rolling out the dough in the cellar while I served the customers upstairs.

I went down when the morning rush was over and apologized to her for the heat of the ovens. We can swap places if you like, I told her. It's awful down here.

To be honest with you, she said, sprinkling some flour with a flourish, her cheeks shining with sweat, it's a nice change not to have to serve people. I get tired of being polite all the time, especially at the moment. She patted her stomach. Everybody wants to tell me what I should be doing, what I should be eating, now it's finally happened. If I go up and serve the bread they'll probably tell me it's unlucky and the baby will come out with raisins for eyes. Can't you keep me hidden down here forever? She smiled at me, dimples cutting deep through her flushed face.

My husband kept his back to us, silent as usual. Briefly I wished I could take his place, stand beside her with my hands in the dough, talking about normal things, like who was angry at who and who was sick or pretending to be and what interesting thing we'd just heard from the neighbouring towns. Not starving for contact, lying beside my husband in our silent bedroom, or glutting myself on unspeakable secrets at Violet's house.

If you're sure, I said, leaving them to it, secretly relieved, as it really was very warm. Upstairs in the shop alone, I folded my arms on the counter and rested my head for a moment.

The children were already gathering wood, let out early from school to forage whatever they could, building vast piles in the shorn field where we would gather. I listened to them running past the shop, shouting at each other. The bell above the door roused me as Mme G came in, muttering something unintelligible to herself. Get me a seat, she said. This heat is unbearable, I need to sit down. What are you doing, sleeping?

I brought my stool round the counter for her and she lowered herself onto it. She stuck out her legs from her long black skirt, veins roping across white skin. They were fascinatingly ugly. She saw me looking and shook one at me. Get an eyeful! she crowed, then groaned. Oh, my back hurts from washing that bitch's clothes. They're so delicate, the grime gathers in all the embroidery, so much work. My spine will never recover. And if my back hurts, my legs hurt. Can I have some bread?

Are you going to pay for it? I eyed her wearily.

Pay for it? she said. Elodie, I'm almost dead. The least you can do is give me something to eat so I can meet my maker with a full stomach. Besides, I have gossip.

You always have gossip, I said, wrapping a loaf. Who would have thought it of someone so pious?

You're one to talk, she said. She slapped her knee. Anyway. I saw a car come through the town at midnight, later even. Just last night. A very fancy car, a green one. It was going towards the ambassador's house! And then later on I heard it drive back, hours afterwards. It must have been someone visiting them, but at that time?

You probably dreamed it, I said. How could you have seen all that in the middle of the night? I handed her the parcel of bread and she held it like a baby. Why were you awake, anyway?

When you get to my age, you won't sleep either, she said. The moon was very bright last night, Elodie. I know what I saw.

Well, it's a story, I'm sure, but I don't think it qualifies as gossip, I said.

Use your head! Who travels at midnight unless they've got something to hide? I've never liked them, not since the day they arrived. Oh, hello, she said then, and I turned to see the grocer's wife coming up the stairs with a tray of tarts.

Husband not working you hard enough? Come over here then, she said, and the grocer's wife reluctantly presented herself so that Mme G could set down the loaf and grip onto her thickening waist instead. She rolled her eyes at me as the old lady placed her face close to her stomach and listened intently.

Too early to tell whether it's a girl or boy, she said, letting go after some concentration.

You don't say, said the grocer's wife. Elodie, I've got to get back. She kissed my cheeks and took off her apron, handed it to me.

Wait! I said, as she stepped away. In spite of the apron, there were floured fingerprints all over her from where she had absent-mindedly wiped her hands. I brushed them off her back and waist. I'm so sorry, it gets everywhere, I said, but she only shrugged graciously.

I've been in worse states. I'll see you two tomorrow, she said. Bye, Georgette.

Mme G heaved herself off her stool. Watch out for more midnight visitors, I said to her.

Oh, piss off, she said. She held up the loaf. Thanks for this.

I waved her off and laid my head on the counter once more.

We closed early the next day, selling out before lunchtime. The tarts and brioche were very good. Not as good as I could have made, I said to my husband. But she's got a light touch. Maybe she'll be after my job. I wouldn't mind swapping. You know she eats sweets all day in that place, I could go for that.

He hardly shrugged. Anger surged inside me, hot and clean. Perhaps I'll kill myself and she can run the bakery, perhaps I'll throw myself off the bridge or bake myself into a pie, what do you think? I said, in the same bright tone. He shrugged again and left the room.

I lipsticked my mouth for the festival, even though I knew the heat of the fire would melt the make-up straight off. I wore the new blue dress I had bought with Violet too, risking the streaks of soot. Nobody would be looking at me so what did it matter anyway, I thought grimly. I might as well wear them and enjoy them. I wasn't dead yet.

It was a clear afternoon, dry and hot. The young people had done well with building the bonfires. Out in the fields beyond the town, tables had been laid, covered in red-and-white gingham and festooned with flowers, lines and lines of bottles of wine and glasses. The butcher and his sons had set up their own smaller fire and a stall, roasting whole pigs one by one on a spit. I never liked this part, the pig thrust undignified on the spike with an expression almost of surprise, but the hot meat and fat pressed between slices of bread was too good to miss. Too good to eat slowly, too good not to almost choke upon. I wondered sometimes if I would ever have a normal appetite again, or if the knowledge of hunger, and how flimsy the things that kept us from hunger were, would always be there underneath. The thin booklet with the eggs and milk and flour marked in a sober column, stretched through the week, kept in the kitchen drawer with our passports and a faded marriage certificate.

The band set up to play with their fiddles, men from the town headed up by the barkeeper. When they started the first song, there was a rustle of interest from the milling crowd, and I saw that there was a new player among them, holding a finer instrument than the others, well oiled and cared for. It was the ambassador.

He plays the fiddle? exclaimed a voice behind me, and I turned around to see Mme F, already holding a bun from the butcher's stall, wearing a stiff cotton dress I remembered from the last festival. Who would have thought? she said to me. She lifted the sandwich to her mouth and bit, seeming not to notice the slick of oil sliding down her wrist.

But how does he know the songs? I asked. She shrugged, wiped her mouth with the heel of her hand.

Everybody knows the songs, she said. She seemed to inspect me more closely then, taking in the dress, the lipstick, and she whistled. You look very nice. Let's get a drink.

Permission was what we needed, in that town where things had fallen and been rebuilt, where the bridge stretched across the water and reminded us that some things could last forever, but only if they were made of stone, and even then not always. Permission had been in short supply, and we were still getting used to it. The sense of relief was palpable.

Josie's driving me to distraction, Mme F said to me. I'm going to drink until I'm sick. She's always out of the house, never watching her brothers when she's supposed to be. She told me the other day she was watching the shop for you, she said you're having headaches, is she telling the truth? Is she lying again?

She is watching it sometimes, I said. My head isn't always good at the moment. I appreciate her help.

Show me the pain, Mme F said. I pointed vaguely at the front of my head.

That's normal, she said, pouring a glass of wine for each of us. I'd be worried if you had no pain at all.

We drank swiftly. It felt good. I was seeing everything as if in new colour—the young girls kneeling or sprawled in the long grass away from the crowd, making flower crowns, crates of wine carried up from the town and yet more barrels of beer being rolled towards tables, the smoke streaming into the sky and stinging my eyes already—but I couldn't see Violet anywhere. Mme F had launched into another complaint about Josette, how she would stop talking for days at a time, like an anchoress taking a vow of silence. If she wants to be a nun so badly I'll send her away, see how much she likes that, she said. She's sluttish, she takes after her father. I nodded, only half listening, craning my neck, searching for a glimpse of Violet, hanging around the band or moving lightly through the crowd.

Here she is, Mme F said suddenly. Josie! Josette! she shouted. Oh no, don't you pretend you didn't hear that, you're deaf now too? You're going to put me in an early grave.

Josette came to us, reluctantly. Mama, you make too much fuss, she said. Hello, Elodie.

The girl looked pretty in her white dress, limbs a little too thin, a thick plait of sun-streaked blonde reaching down her back, large white daisies and purple irises wound into a ring around her temples.

Well at least you're talking today, said Mme F. Her hand shot out and grasped Josette's forearm. You be good this evening, you hear me?

I looked away, heard her answer, Yes. She was released.

I don't know who will kill who first, Mme F declared, watching her walk away. Be glad you never had a daughter.

Oh, she's a good girl, I said. You remember what it was like to be young.

I remember nothing, Mme F said, draining her wine. I was certainly not a slut, anyway. We didn't have the opportunity. Another? Clotilde! she shouted, raising her voice again as she spotted the mayor's wife, and I took the opportunity to take my wine and go.

People were drunk already, but cheerful too, red in the face and knocking their glasses together. I looked back and saw Mme F and the mayor's wife already deep in conversation, glancing over in my direction, or just simply looking towards someone in the distance. It's true that on the day of the midsummer festival I felt more keenly my place in the town: I had never been a girl who jumped over the embers or watched the boys jumping over and wondered which one would marry me. No number of their secrets, no amount of accumulated power, would make me one of them; and yet I could not leave, either.

The music was loud and wild. I moved closer to the band to watch the ambassador playing, his shirtsleeves rolled up as if he was just one of the men, just a man who had been there all his life, but his face was so intent on the performance that his mouth almost looked cruel. The sight of his strong grip on the bow made me close my eyes for a second. I opened them to see him watching me, and he winked.

I pushed exultant through the crowd of people eating, drinking, the shadows lengthening behind me. Violet was nowhere to be found, as if she had never existed. I wanted her to see the town like this, when it was most itself, and the two of us together in its undeniable midst, neither of us belonging. People were dancing in earnest now, in pairs, the crowd gathering around them. Two women toasted one another as they passed, swinging around, and as their glasses hit together they shattered—the women shrieked as wine and glass went everywhere. I wanted to dance alone, to raise my arms up above my head and close my eyes and sway, but the grocer took me by the elbows as if catching me from a fall and then swung me out and I let myself be moved, the darkening sky eddying, filled with sparks.

He moved his mouth to my ear. Where's Marie? he asked, shouting over the fiddles.

I shook my head to indicate I didn't know. He was compact in his white shirt, twirling me neatly.

Never mind, he said. She always turns up somewhere!

He laughed as if he had made a great joke, and released me into the arms of someone else, the mayor this time, his head shining with perspiration and his gold medallion around his neck, because it was a special day.

Elodie! he bellowed, like he hadn't seen me in years.

We spun around until I started to feel sick. I thought I glimpsed my husband watching in the clapping crowd around us, dragged away by the dance too fast to see, and when I looked again he was gone.

Watch out! the mayor said, pointing at the ground, where a pair of green-and-brown adders were shimmering across the ground. They must have been sleeping in the woodpile, woken by the heat and the smoke. The crowd jumped nimbly to let them pass. They want to dance as well! he laughed.

At that I had to wrench myself away, pushing through the ring of people surrounding us, hands patting me and voices calling my name. Don't leave us now, Elodie! they said. The main dances are just about to start! But I couldn't stay.

Down by the lake, the sound of the festival distant from two fields away, I leaned against a tree and cried without really knowing why. Though it was too dark to see, I felt surreptitious movements of bodies around me, the sound of my misery driving them away in panic, and I wanted to tell them to stay, stay—lie down in the churned-up earth, do what you want, none of it means anything.

I must have stood there for an hour or more, watching the sky darkening. The dancing had stopped by the time I returned, picking my way through livid mud, my shoes ruined and the hem of my dress filthy. At the outskirts of the crowd, I paused, taking in the newly solemn atmosphere. The main bonfire was still burning bright, but the crowd's attention had moved to one of the smaller ones, only glowing embers left. Gradually a silence fell as we watched the teenagers, boys and girls both, line up facing it.

We remained silent as the first boy stepped forward from the line, paused, then broke into a run. He ran straight towards the embers, sprinting as fast as he could go, clearing the heat effortlessly in one long jump. Only once he had touched down on the ground did we allow ourselves to cheer, lapsing back into expectant silence as soon as the next figure readied to run. It was the butcher's youngest son—too young to be courting, old enough not to want to miss the fun, and with his gangly legs he cleared it easily too. The crowd sighed with relief but I could sense it growing a little restless. Perhaps the fire was too small this year, not enough of a challenge.

Josette went third, her skirts knotted up above her knees to avoid catching flame, which I was sure she would get into trouble for later. When she landed safe on the other side she got the biggest cheer yet. We turned back to the waiting line, the crowd looking as one. Shuffling forward was a group of boys I didn't recognize, probably from the next town over. Boys in neighbouring towns would often hear about the festivities, coming for the girls and the food and the sneaked glasses of wine, but they didn't usually jump. I watched the first unfamiliar boy ready himself, half-visible in the glow from the dying fire. He must have been about fifteen or so, soft-featured, dark-haired.

Who's that? I heard the mayor's wife ask behind me, and an unintelligible answer from someone.

Thick silence again as he started to run. But at the last moment he veered off, away from the embers, and kept on running. We turned to see him heading towards the bigger bonfire, and with one graceful leap, no hesitation, he jumped right into its heart. And in the moment before I screamed, mine just another among everybody else's screams, there was a strange sense of rightness, of homecoming—a sense that underneath all the wine and dancing and forgetting, this was what we had really come to see.

It's important to remember that, despite past catastrophes, our world was undeniably good. The fruit crops in the outlying farms mostly grew well, trees heavy with red cherries. Tourists came to look at the famous bridge, with their shining cars and their money to spend in the cafés and restaurants and bars, and sent postcards home. Deep blue of the sky against the long river, pale streets and alleys of stone, the heat perfect in the morning, burning all the badness away. I see it now like a photograph, or a painting, saccharine with its own mythology.

Violet was a painter herself, though as far as I know she never painted the town, or anything that happened in it, past or present. No dogs in nets, no fighter jets, no ancient bridge, no burning boy. When I told her about the terrible accident at the festival she barely seemed to register it, as if the outside world was irrelevant. I could never predict what would fascinate her and what would leave her bored, irritable. She painted flowers and still lifes, decorative and inanimate, like the ones she had to do in the art classes at her convent school, ten girls in white dresses studying pears on a sheet. Just once she showed me a sketchbook from before she got married, which was entirely different, full of women holding their heads serenely in their hands, strange rabbits with the faces of babies.

No more of that now, she told me.

Why not? I asked, and she just tilted her head and smiled at me.

Wouldn't you like to know, she said.

The first time she drew my hands I did not notice, she did it so quickly, stealthily. We were sitting half-asleep in the thick heat, in the courtyard at the back of the shop, a stolen hour on one of the hottest days of the year. She had come to see me for once.

It stinks out here, Violet said. I don't see how you could possibly doze off. Anyway, look.

She turned the sketchbook around to face me. My hands—burned against hot metal, weathered by water. They hid nothing. I was ashamed to see them and told her so.

No, they're beautiful, she told me. Real hands, hands that have done real things.

I hated her for that, actually, and I silently begged her to say more things like that, to give me fewer reasons to love her, to stoke my scorn until it burned me out of helplessness, I already knew that nothing else would do it.

Was it truly beautiful to her, any of it? When she walked around our pretty town did she feel a kind of peace, or was it more a strangulation, that feeling of a hot thread around the throat, constricting the breath? Did she lean against doorways, catch glimpses of shadow in these places where she could breathe for a second, listening to the bells as they chimed on the quarter-hour, the matrons dressed in dark and light cottons, hair covered, the children racing along the pavement? The sun high in the air. Did she stumble home, stricken by the life visible to her underneath this life, the water beneath the surface? Or did she watch us calmly, make eye contact with a passing man before looking away, turn back to see him still looking, stop in at the grocer's store to hold an apple cool and heavy in her palm, drop a little word into the pretty wife's ear, and watch me through the plate glass as she walked past? Did she see me wrapping bread in paper and scrutinizing the worn skin of my hands, and what did she think—*there you are*—oblivious with my mouth pursed in a quiet tuneless hum, caught off guard, *poor Elodie*. Perhaps she walked to the square and sat there with her apple and considered her options, what portion of herself to dole out next and to whom.

The frequency of my neighbours' confessions ticked up through the summer, as if the heat brought out something in them, made them long to lose their secrets like too-heavy clothes.

I didn't mean to hurt her.

I wish she'd hurry up and die.

I've dreamed the same thing three times in a week. I'm starting to see it even when my eyes are open.

I'm plotting my revenge.

I know he's following me.

Sometimes I wake up and everything is blue.

I'll kill her rather than give him up.

It's not his.

It's not mine.

The confessions were giving me less and less pleasure. Maybe I was too full of the things that Violet told me to have room for anything else. When I shut my eyes I saw the boy in the fire; I saw the ambassador holding his fiddle lovingly against his shoulder, drawing the bow effortlessly downwards.

One evening not long after the festival, when I was sorting

through my husband's soiled clothes, I felt something heavy in the breast pocket of his baking smock. It was small and hard, a tube of some kind, like a lipstick, and my heart dropped, then leapt—evidence at last. But when I pulled the object out it was not make-up, at least not obviously so. It was a small, glass jar with a metal screw top, unmarked and filled with liquid. I tried to twist off the lid but it was stuck fast, and I was afraid of breaking it. I slipped the bottle into my pocket and carried on.

My husband returned from the bar many hours later. He was spending most nights there by that point. Hot orange light, beer and wine spilled on the tables. You're awake, he said when he finally came in. I had lit candles around me for the friendliness of their flame, I was sewing but had stopped when I heard his key in the lock. He rested against the frame of the door, watching me then. He walked over to the sink and poured himself a glass of water. How was your evening? I asked. I could tell from his gait that he was drunk.

Nothing to report, he said. The ambassador was in a good mood, buying everybody's drinks.

Why? I asked.

He looked at me irritably. I don't know why, he said. Maybe he was celebrating something. Maybe he came into money, maybe it was his birthday, I didn't ask, I just drank. Should I have interviewed him? By the way, we should have them round for dinner, he said, and I nodded with surprise at his suggestion, thinking of them sitting politely in this house that bread had built, the house I still sometimes felt a stranger in, with its cracks in the plaster and yellowed linen forever needing bleaching and the dark corners where dust accumulated and stuck.

He opened his mouth and then hesitated. I wondered whether

he would finally ask what was wrong with me, or demand to know what I did with Violet during those long afternoons when he noticed me absent from the bakery and never said a word, her hair pulled through my hands.

I've been meaning to tell you something, he said.

I waited.

I saw you before the café, he said, sitting down on the chair next to mine. We only went there because of you.

Which café?

The first time we met, he said. I had seen you before we met in the café. I passed you in the street. You wore your hair long then, if you remember.

He reached out to hover his hand a few inches below my shoulder, where my hair used to fall.

I was just walking around one afternoon, my father was asleep in our hotel room. It wasn't like me, but I turned around and started following you.

He paused to observe my reaction. I didn't know what to say. He had recounted his confession not with fondness, but flatly, as if he had pulled the memory up, with a lot of concentration, from somewhere he rarely went.

You moved as if you had a secret. Maybe I wanted to know what the secret was, he said. Or maybe you were just pretty. A lot of boys would have followed you.

Why didn't you come into the café that same day? I asked him.

I was nervous, he said. And besides, my father probably would have been awake by then, wondering where I was.

There was no secret, I said. You know everything about me.

He smiled uneasily. I could tell I was going too far, pushing on the unfamiliar intimacy like a bruise. I stood up and started to gather my spools of thread, folding squares of cloth, I turned away from him, and he kept talking.

He said, You've settled something for me, which is that I always wondered if you had noticed me following you, because I did it for quite a while, forty minutes maybe, I can't remember. I've been waiting for you to bring it up all these years, I thought you must know, nothing gets past you. But you never saw me doing it.

No, I said. I didn't know. The idea would never have entered my mind.

Hands folding cloth over and over in a circle of candlelight, amber; I felt the old swing of my braid where it had hit the centre of my back, heavy, as if it were still there.

I'm glad, he said.

I wasn't glad. If I had looked behind me and seen his face, recognized the same face in the café the next day, known that there was a moment in my life when he had noticed me and followed me along a pavement clean with damp spring rain, would it have changed my marriage? To have lived knowing this one thing. Young Elodie, not yet serene or grimly familiar, hurrying back to my room where another sweet country girl slept in a single bed a metre away from mine. And somewhere in the world was Violet, perhaps even still in the mountainous landscape of her schooldays, back then, very far away indeed.

In the early days of our marriage, we did everything expected of us. I washed our bedclothes in the lavoir while the older women looked knowingly on. Memory fails me here out of marriage's familiarity; memory lessens the sweetness, tells me it was never so good, but I know at one time, even if only for one night, one hour even, there was pleasure. There must have been. I can't lose the memory of myself on a sheet laid cool and flat with my husband above me, the husband I found beautiful, the release of my body as it bucked, then stilled. I can't forget that before anything else there was the promise of a town of pale stone and a beautiful bridge. I fell into this life, I was not thrown.

Remembering these things sparked a strange resentment in me, reminded me of how far we had wandered from the place we started. I found something in your pocket today, I said. I drew the miniature bottle out from my skirt and set it on the table between us. He leaned forward, lifted his hands, and I thought he might take mine in his, but instead he placed them on his knees.

Well?

It's the additive, the one they use in America. The ambassador sourced it for me.

I stared at him, speechless at the smallness of his secrets. He felt more for his bread than he would ever feel for me.

Yes, it's a risk, he continued, addressing himself as much as me. It's not been approved here. Yes, it's a risk, he said again, as if talking himself into something.

We contemplated the bottle together.

But the bread could be the best it's ever been. The greatest bread in the country, he said.

I saw the light in his eyes and softened a little. Imagined the pavement crammed with strangers, with competitors, the cars parked nose to tail along the verge, the people thronging the bridge, all for the miraculous bread, *Body of Christ*. I leaned forward and took his hands, and in my own hands they felt like stone.

You should do it, I told him. We deserve it, I told him.

I don't know, he said. I'm still working it out. Please don't get ahead of yourself, Elodie. He pulled his hands back and then frowned. You've been quite strange this summer, he said. I don't know what's become of you.

I'm still myself, I said. It's still me.

The idea of the perfect bread excited me, the shared secret. I stood up and my hands went to the buttons at the back of my neck, started to undo them.

It's probably too much of a risk, he said, ignoring the loosening of the fabric around my neck, ignoring me as I peeled the dress downwards until it was at my waist.

It was kind of him to get it for you, I said. He must think of you as a friend. (*I know you want to fuck him.*) I unhooked my brassiere, dropped it on the floor like it was a dead animal, an offering.

I have to say that I didn't think much of him at first, he said. But he's really changed my mind. He's one of us at heart. An honest sort.

It could change our lives, I said, fighting the urge to put my hands on my nakedness, to hide behind them. I took a step forward and knelt before him, reaching for his belt, but he put his hand on mine.

Come here, he said. Turn around.

I sat on the floor with his knees against my back and leaned into him as if he were a chair, with relief. I felt his hands at the nape of my neck, and there they rested for a moment, his thumbs gentle on my vertebrae, before they pulled the material of my dress back up over my shoulders and started to fasten the buttons.

I don't know what's become of you, he said again, but this time kindly. Hot water stung my eyes. Hot band of ribbon at my throat where the fabric was tight once more, burning. He put his lips to the crown of my head.

Dear Violet,

Long before I met you, I felt that if I could only get to beauty, something speechless and formless would be absolved in me—if I could only get beyond my own hands lathered in soap, chapped from flour and coins, hands which did not touch or receive touch, hands sewing by a circle of lamplight. I didn't have the language for it then, in fact I tried not to think about it at all. Of course I know now that beauty is relative. Now I can pine for the swallows nesting in the roof of the lavoir, the dry dirt and grass under my feet, the river's winding path. Even a newly mopped flagstone, butter melting on potatoes, a mended white cloth to shake out over a table and set with things gleaming sharp and bright.

Perhaps I miss the lavoir most of all. My circle of women is gone; Mme F is still in the asylum, Mme G is dead, Josette too. I wash my clothes in the basin of my sink, under the bare ceiling bulb. But the suds still soften the water, and my clothes hang around the room like flags, steaming. Living bodies continue. They sweat, they bleed, they drip coffee on their skirts. They cry until the linen of their dour blouses crinkles stiff and unruly with salt.

Something in Violet started to show. Something in the gleam of her eyes, her hair which grew longer, the ambassador forbidding her to cut it as he wound it around his hand and pulled. Like this, she showed me one afternoon in her bedroom, wrapping my own around hers.

Sometimes I think there's another animal growing underneath my skin, she said then. Do you know what I mean?

I think that's nonsense, I told her, running my own fingers along the bony knobs at the top of her shoulders. My hair was still wrapped around her hand and she tugged, lightly.

I'm going to draw you again, she told me strictly, letting go. Don't bother saying you don't want me to, because I know you do. I've got everything ready.

She darted over to her dressing table, seizing a curved white jug of opalescent milk-glass which I hadn't seen before.

See what nice things I have found for you?

She dragged the chair onto the red rug in the centre of the room. Sit there and don't move, she told me. She went downstairs and I tried to track the movement of her body through the floor, to sense the pattern of her heat radiating through the house. She came back in holding a pair of wilting sunflowers. She placed one in the jug, and then she handed it to me. It was surprisingly heavy.

Hold it out like this, she said, moving my arm like an inanimate object, perpendicular to my left side; it began to ache at once. She put her cool hands on my face, tilting my head back, then tucking my hair behind my ear. On her hands and knees she positioned my legs and feet precisely, crossing one foot over the other. I let myself be manipulated, and gladly, though it occurred to me that it would be very easy to kick her when she was prostrated like that, kick her hard, and pretend it was an accident. I could even get her chin, I thought—break her jaw entirely.

She settled herself back on the bed with her sketchbook. It was strange how quickly I got used to it, the watching which turned from intrusion into a kind of intimacy. She seemed to take the same care observing the lines of the jug as she did my body, or at least I watched her for some kind of pleasure when she looked directly at me, the pleasure of recording a beloved thing, and saw no such change in her expression. My arm hurt—soon it was all I could think of—but I did not move. I wondered if she had picked the jug on purpose for that reason. When she put the sketch-pad down, I tried not to let her see what a relief it was to stretch and bend my limbs, setting the jug carefully on the floor.

Let's do another one, she said. Come on, get up. She moved the chair to the side of the room. Now sit down on the rug.

I arranged myself awkwardly, ankles crossed like a child. Violet crouched down then to twist my body one way and my legs another, one bent and one stretched long, my face in profile. Both flowers this time, she said, moving my arms out in front of me, stretched out straight, and placing a sunflower in each hand. This too was uncomfortable, even more uncomfortable than before. It took great effort to keep my body upright at all. That's perfect, she said. You look so wonderful, Elodie. Just perfect.

I couldn't watch her draw me from this new position. I was looking straight towards the cupboard, could see the reflection of myself dimly in the polished wood of the door, watery and distorted. The stems of the sunflowers were strangely fleshy, bristly, and made my skin itch. I clutched them tighter to try to distract myself from the discomfort radiating through my body.

Eventually she released me again. She smiled. One more, she said.

The chair returned and I sat on it with my knees pressed close together. She balanced the jug on my head, empty. Stay very still, she said, serious. The urge to move was overwhelming. After a few minutes I shut my eyes tight in order to concentrate. My hands gripped the seat of the chair, I kept my neck rigid. Open your eyes, she said, and a few seconds later, with sickening inevitability, I felt the jug slip and fall to the floor, though I hadn't moved at all, or didn't think I had. It broke into four large pieces, as clean as something sliced. I picked them up with shaking hands and put them on the seat of the chair.

I'm sorry, I said. She didn't seem to hear me. I'm sorry, Violet, I said again.

That's enough for today, she said. And then she was silent for a long time, flicking through the pages of her sketchbook while I stood before her, wretched. But when I turned to go, she started speaking.

My husband surprised me yesterday. I was in the bath—well, almost.

I bit my lip, then turned back around. She smiled placidly.

(I know you're in there, he said. The steam filled the room.

I'm drawing a bath, she called back, then relented and went to the door. He smelled sharp and medicinal. She pressed her face to his neck to smell for perfume, she pulled his hands to her face and kissed his fingertips, she put his fingers in her mouth, and he drew his hand away, started to pull up her dress. She resisted and he broke off, bending down to take the glass of wine from where she had left it, on the floor next to the bath. Where were you? she asked, combative. He had been gone all evening. He laughed and carried on, fingers hooked into her underwear, pulling it down. I was everywhere, he told her.

The water was still hot afterwards. She climbed in, let herself sink under the surface and stay there for a few seconds as he remained beside her, sitting on the floor, still clothed. Opened her eyes to blurred light, came back up, drank half of the wine in the glass and then passed it to him. She looked at him closely as he swallowed, his throat tipped up. Her hair was plastered to her head. Serpent-woman, otherworldly, soon her ribs would shine through her skin and then her lungs and her heart too, everything about her too close to the surface and uncontainable.

I can't tell if we are at the point where a good love turns bad, if we already passed it, or if it is up ahead for them still at this point. I don't know really where love begins, though I've been trying to pin it down, and I know even less where it ends.

He took up the sponge and frothed it with soap, then raised her nearest arm and cleaned her, gently, from the top of her shoulder to her hand. He soaped each finger in turn and did the same for her leg, her cherry-red toenails. No resistance from her, though no indication that she was enjoying it either. Her ankle was small in his hand, and he thought, briefly, about breaking it—one clean twist to the left, like snapping a chicken's neck.

He gestured for her to turn and he washed her the same way on the other side. Sweat beaded her forehead from the heat. He scolded her for the state of her fingernails, sweetly, like she was a child. Get in, she told him then, and he did. She reclined against his chest, the white cotton of his shirt soaked through. Her heart beat like a bird's through her back and he could feel it, too fast. She sat up and he raised his wet hand, held it in front of him like a greeting, and she leaned her head back into the grip, like a brace after an accident. Her hair hung to the water; she closed her eyes, sighed. The two of them stayed like that for a long while, like acrobats, balanced in a strange embrace. There were no lights on in the house. The water went cold. The town was hollowed out. Not even the stray dogs roamed the streets. Afterwards she lay naked on the bed in front of him, calm and pale, and he just looked, and she fell asleep under his gaze.)

As if her story had conjured him up, we heard the door click downstairs and his footsteps in the hall. Quiet, quiet up the stairs. He smiled to see me there in their room. I was brushing Violet's hair quite innocently. Can I borrow my wife? he asked. Of course I followed them down the stairs. Crouched on the staircase, peering down through the open door to the dining room, I saw him set a glass of water in front of her. She was facing away from me, arms crossed; I saw her fingers move nervously over her elbows, as if she was cringing from the cold. I watched as he raised a glass medicine dropper and added a single teardrop of fluid to the tumbler, then sheathed the dropper back in a small dark vial. Go on, he said. It's good for you.

She paused another second, then picked up the glass and swallowed its contents in one. Go and tell Elodie that she has to go home, she said.

I scrambled back up the stairs and sat hastily on the edge of the bed, knees pressed together. When he entered the room he had the air of an executioner. He sat beside me, heavily.

Sorry to drag her away from you like that, Elodie. I didn't mean to appear abrupt, but it was urgent. He set his hands on his thighs. I wanted to thank you, he said then, unexpectedly. You're very good for her. Look, you don't have to come here just out of obligation. I know she can be a bit of a handful. I don't recall her ever having a friend before.

It's no obligation, I said.

He smiled. I don't know what this town would do without you. Everyone always says it.

They do? I asked, stunned.

You're very loved here, he said. Anybody can see it. He put his hand on mine, briefly.

At the lavoir the women were subdued. There was no more trying on of Violet's clothes, no more playful interrogations. It was cool between the eaves above us and the reflection of the eaves below, even as it grew hotter by the day. Flickering light against the underside of the roof. I held my wrists underwater longer than was necessary and visualized my blood cooling. I longed to climb in and hold my whole body under the surface, to watch the slow movement of the soap where it beaded the water above me. Mme G sang from time to time, a strange crooning that put me on edge. Josette was quiet and pale, tethered to the eyeline of her mother. I twisted and pulled wet fabric and imagined it was Violet between my hands, her hair, her throat, pliable yet heavy; whether to hurt or seduce I couldn't tell, there seemed no difference there, in the unreal green light.

Every day, sex clung more thickly to her and couldn't be scrubbed away. I saw her pass the window of the bakery and imagined her sensing the eyes on her as she walked with her head bowed, only to look up and find nobody to meet her gaze. The men saw it; she told me the butcher was almost rude to her, lecherous, bloody hands moving too close to hers. She couldn't look away from how the crimson sunk into his callused skin. He never wore gloves because he wanted to feel the way the meat gave in to him, the weight and heft of each specific cut. It's respectful to the animal, he told my husband, as they compared trades. To acknowledge that what is in your hands was once a living creature in a world of its own. Thoughts, feelings. These men, drunk on their mythologies. She told me how the hams and legs hanging around her head, the little skinned rabbits with their paws up as if begging, made her feel sick. She took the meat in its greaseproof paper, put it in her basket. He told her to give his regards to her husband. The butcher was a fan of his. At night they often sat together in the bar and drank until the butcher's face was red, the ambassador mirroring his joviality, slapping him lightly on the arm. The men talked to him about their wives, complained, confided, no doubt including my husband. I don't believe the ambassador talked about Violet, though. He would have smiled and stayed silent as the others goaded, became coarse and ribald, waited for them to blunder into their own traps.

I started to take bread when I went to see her. I wanted her to eat it, I wanted to see it move down her throat. I tried so many loaves, a different recipe every time, to tempt her. In my kitchen I experimented with twisting dough into appealing shapes, or pressing in raisins and nuts. I tried caraway seeds, cinnamon, loaves enriched with milk and egg, with cheese, with green olives. My hands would squeeze the dough like flesh as I went again and again over the evidence (*If you eat the bread, you'll die*), which perhaps meant nothing and was just a misheard line, a misunderstanding (*I know you want to fuck him*).

Don't think me rude, she said, time and time again, as I showed her my offerings, arranged them on the red-bordered china plates with a rose in the centre, and she would win—I would eat the bread myself in the end, broken by her hands into ragged pieces, they were my sacrament.

But in the baking I found myself closer to answers, if there were any, in the meditative act of handling the dough. Be there, I told myself. I remembered the slip of light, the blue bead lost between the floorboards, and maybe he was not prostrating himself before her but had his hands up her skirt, and maybe when his hand was at her throat it was a game they were playing, and his words after all had been muffled in the cloth of her skirt, perhaps he had stuffed his mouth with it so as not to cry out in pain or pleasure, and I didn't know how long my husband had been next to me, watching too, seemingly unmoved, but maybe he knew more than I knew, maybe he knew the meaning of *If you eat the bread, you'll die* and of *I know you want to fuck him*, because both of these statements seemed to be about him, while neither of them were about me. I would have led her into my own bedroom gladly if she had wanted it, as long as I could stay in the corner to watch her and my husband, not hidden in a sliver of light but there, a known spectator, to see my bed made new, my husband made new, the humiliation of my inability made delicious, on the edge of my chair to take it all in.

Late-summer thunderstorm, the wind high all morning and getting higher. My husband had finally mentioned Josette the week before, and I had said something vague about my headaches, but I didn't know how many more stolen days I could spend with Violet. I felt wretched, frantic at even the idea of the loss.

When the clock struck midday I wrapped up a simple baguette

and left the shop anyway, not caring if anybody else would come. At her kitchen table, Violet sat, barely moving. She left the bread untouched, didn't even bother to rip it up.

Can I just go back to bed, do you think? I can't bear it today. I've had more than enough.

I trailed her upstairs, cautious. She took up her sketchpad, began to draw her own face in the dressing-table mirror, then immediately set the charcoal down again.

I'll never be more than this, she said. Sometimes I feel like I'll never leave this place. This is all busywork, it passes the time. That's all I want, now. The time to be passed until he's back with me, and then my real life begins again.

I glanced around the room for inspiration, something to entertain her with. There was always something new in the bedroom, by that point. A small leather ball that she would toss, absently, then put in her mouth like an apple to demonstrate—glossy with her saliva when she removed it, her lips wet. A footstool, a poker, a chair.

Violet came to sit by me, on the bed, propped up by cushions. She was wearing the necklace, some kind of code for whatever game was being played that day, in the part of her life that didn't involve me. Her hand, cool, found mine. Her legs, naked under her dress, her red-tipped feet.

The room was dark and the wind hurled rain against the panes over and over. Her eyes were glowing, glowing. Do I seem myself? she asked.

Instead of answering, I went downstairs to get us more drinks. I remembered the dropper, the spiked water, and I opened the cupboards, searching for the glass vial I had seen in the ambassador's hand. Behind a bag of sugar, I found three identical vials, two still sealed, none labelled. Medicine, I told myself. Probably nothing more than gripe water, or rose petals distilled with sugar. It warmed my heart to imagine myself and the ambassador guarding Violet, sickly and strange with no friends in the world. It was the happiest I had felt all week. I pictured her vomiting into a bowl, two points of colour high on her cheeks, asking me weakly never to leave her, and I smiled and unscrewed the cap of the nearest vial, drew out the dropper and put four drops in her wine glass. I replaced it carefully, so that he wouldn't know what I had done, though I was sure he would welcome my initiative. I took the bottle of wine and the glasses upstairs.

When I returned, Violet seemed distracted, agitated even. Tell me a story, she said. Tell me one interesting thing about this place.

I sat facing her, holding her gaze from the foot of the bed. All right, I said.

I told her about the river which ran right through the town and which had once borne the dead back to us, fidgeting with a silk ribbon as I spoke, twining it between my fingers. I never saw them, but my mother-in-law swore it was true. If I was going to be part of this place, I needed to know these things, she had told me, as if her town wasn't the same as every other town. There was a cold night in the dead of winter, the water froze over, and the dead came up the river on this bridge of ice and walked into the town. It was a rare moment of peace between calamities, and the dead stepped into that peace. Mothers, fathers, friends, lovers, lost children. Some were recognized and some were not but all had belonged to someone, once. They walked along the streets and then into the houses, into bars and cafés, like they had never left. They were not grotesque. They looked like anyone else, except for the eyes, blue and ringed with dark circles. If you touched their skin, they were freezing, but if you touched their skin you died. Not then, necessarily, but later. If you touched their skin a ghost of you walked back with them when they left the town hours later, still walking on the river though it had thawed by morning. It separated those who were willing to embrace from those who were not. Those who were not afraid of death and so would touch it, pull it closer to their body.

But it's not true, of course, I told her. Only children would believe in it.

But what about your mother-in-law? she countered. She saw what she saw.

There was a clarity in this that stilled me. *She saw what she saw.* We could both see it then, I think. The crowd gathered on the banks of the river, watching in silence as the dead walked away, those silver versions of themselves leaving with them. I wondered if you would feel the lack in yourself, a cleaving, when your own ghost disappeared from sight. I shook my head. I tried to stay in the room, there with her, the mattress sagging underneath us. The dust spiralling above in the weak light from the bulb. But I was back in the early days of my marriage again, mired in all that fragile hope. My husband, smiling at me in the morning as he smoothed the hair from my brow. Learning the rhythms of how we loved each other and the bakery both, standing solemn and proud at the till, wrapping the bread with my mother-in-law. Vicious old bitch. I was glad she was dead now too, no longer skulking around the place, cataloguing my lack. I leaned my arm over the side of the bed and let the ribbon drop to the floor.

My mother died before I was born, Violet said, childlike suddenly, uncertain. But she loved me.

I nodded, before realizing it wasn't possible, and looked at her with wariness.

I don't mean died literally, she said. I know you would understand though, sweet Elodie. She loved me very much. You remind me of her.

What about your husband's mother? I asked. Your mother-in-law.

She was silent for a while. We don't see them any more, she said. He's had a hard life, though you might not think it. He fought, of course, though I didn't know him then.

She sat up properly, looked sideways at me. You can't imagine how he suffered. He's seen the evil that human beings are capable of enacting upon each other, she said. I know that can be hard for most people to come to terms with about him. But it might be that you need people less after that, knowing what they're capable of. He has me, and that's enough.

We'll see, I found myself thinking, almost disturbed by my own bottomless hunger even at a moment like this.

Violet slept then, or seemed to, lying down with her eyes closed and her cheek pillowed on her hand. Unsupervised in their home, I left the bedroom and walked along the corridor. On the stairs I sat down for a moment, mesmerized by the swirling, the eddying, of the dust. It spun golden and cloying. I found pan and broom and bucket in the kitchen, swept the stairs and then the hall, casting the glittering dirt out through the back door. The shock of the light, when the door was opened; it was warm, the rain had passed and left the air clean and still, I could hear the mild voices of people passing by. The blue light of early evening. I came back in and opened all the kitchen windows wide. Then I cleaned the pots and pans with their scraps of food, even mould, breathing in great gulps of that air from the world outside to sustain me, to help me remember which world was which. I felt quite strange. It was soothing to get onto my hands and knees as I scrubbed the flagstones, first taking off my dress and hanging it on a hook, so it would not get dirty. She came down and found me there, half-naked, close to the ground in a pool of water. She put a hand on the wall to steady herself.

Get up, get up, she said. She was agitated again. You can't do this.

I stood in front of her in the flesh-coloured underwear which made my body look strangely featureless.

Can you hear footsteps upstairs? she asked me, and for a second, I could.

The ambassador appeared at the bakery the next day, as I was closing for the lunch break. He had never set foot in there before, though perhaps he watched from afar, looking for my body framed in the window. I felt clumsy, unfamiliar, my face flushing hot.

Would you like to buy some bread?

He shook his head.

Would you like coffee? I can go along to the house, or get you something to eat, I offered.

But he didn't want coffee, or anything to eat. He patted his stomach, still mostly flat. I'm not as young as I used to be, he said. I have to watch my appetite now. He looked pale, I noticed. Worn out by something, by the demands Violet made of him, by the things he demanded of her. Which of them was sucking the other's blood? I was inclined to think it was her.

Do you want to see where we make the bread? I asked, finally, and at this he nodded.

In the cellar the oven was still hot. Stone walls pearled with moisture, barrels and bags of flour and yeast and salt. Scratching from the mice in the walls, light. Fresh aprons hanging on the wall like deflated bodies. It must be unbearable when the oven is lit, he said. I wanted to get onto my knees and tell him *yes, it is unbearable*. Instead I just showed him the metal trays with their patina of years of heat, as if I were a tour guide.

Something's been on my mind, he said to me. I've felt quite bad about it, so I wanted to confess. He smiled sheepishly. We lied about how we met, he said. At the party. We have a tradition of making up stories about it—we tell a new one every time. It's foolish, I know, but the truth is terribly boring. I found her in a café, sitting alone, like she was just waiting for me to collect her. He laughed. You can see why I'd rather try to jazz it up with a murder?

(Her pale face like the slip of the moon in the dark café. Nails bitten down to bloody on elegant hands; that sugar, everywhere, crystalline, on the table in front of her. Hair to her shoulders. I see the gleaming prism of it, so many angles at once. Her through me then her through him, ice-cold, though inside she was burning up.)

I knew she needed me, he said. Needed my help.

He stepped forward. He put a hand on my arm. I'm afraid I've told even worse lies about it in the past, he said. It's extraordinary what people will believe. Sometimes I tell them she was running for her life, or even that she was a criminal. Sometimes she becomes the murderer, or I do.

He ringed my bare forearm with both his hands. But I thought you were too sensible to believe that. You don't suffer fools gladly. You don't like things to trip you up.

He took one hand from my arm and put it on my waist. His thumb stroked the curve of my hip. I stayed very still, hardly breathing.

Why do you do it? I asked.

He shrugged, moved his hands away from me cleanly, as if touching me in the first place had been an accident.

Why not? he said. Why not have a little harmless fun where you can.

I felt then that I had displeased him somehow, and at the same time I felt that there was some opportunity in the moment which must not be lost. You must have seen a lot of bad things, I offered. Before, I mean. It must have been awful.

He looked away. You've been discussing me, have you? he said. She's pretty bad at keeping her mouth shut. Fortunately I don't mind you knowing, Elodie. You're an intelligent woman. We all saw bad things.

He looked back at me then, smiled unexpectedly. I think it makes you appreciate beauty more. I've got to go, she'll be wondering where I am. She won't eat if I'm not there, you know how she gets.

Yes, I said. I know how she is.

I followed him up the steps and into the light.

Dear Violet,

Did your husband ever tell you about the times he visited me in
the bakery? Perhaps he would have kept that a secret, or perhaps
you laughed at it together, or perhaps it was so unimportant he
forgot it as soon as it had happened. As I remember it, my skin
turned to dough under his hands—rising, yielding. These are the
sorts of things I see now. No longer being shackled to reality has
its benefits. For instance, he never kissed me, but when I want to I
can imagine it differently, the audacity of memory can be staggering, the liberties I can take and the things I can give myself. His
hot mouth, stubbled, a mouth that could be any man's, really. His
mouth becomes your mouth, the kiss in the dressing room that was
never repeated, your sharp fingernails at the base of my skull. It's
often like this when I'm drunk, the memories slip into each other,
unravel. You are both there, touchable, though I hate myself for it.

Where is the ambassador now, Violet? He's in a beautiful house
somewhere. He's in a prison. He's in a grave. He moves through the
others around him like oil, like a knife through butter. He sits in a

restaurant and orders dinner, chews deliberately. There is a waitress with yellow hair who reminds him of me, a country girl—woman really, older than she first seems—and he asks her what time her shift finishes, and he's there waiting. They walk through the night. He folds her over like paper in a dark alley. The sweet bad smell of the bins nearby. She says yes, she says no, she says nothing. Her heart spills out redly onto her blouse, her blouse remains immaculate white. He marries her, he never sees her again, there's a small moon-faced child with his shock of dark hair, he leaves nothing behind, and he can't do any of this if he's in a grave, though I can't imagine him dead, and I think they would have told me if there was a grave, if he were wrapped in loam, the beautiful bones of his hands bare and no longer grasping, no longer around your throat or mine. Surely they would have told me anything they knew for certain, because the uncertainty fractures and splinters out and destabilizes everything, too many possibilities and realities to bear, like the capacity of a person to be true to you, the capacity of a person to live one good life or several bad ones, and even the more mysterious hours of my husband's life could be accounted for, but then I suppose there are innumerable ways to manipulate reality, I can't know anything with absolute certainty, that has always been the problem. My husband saw me watching him over dinner each night and never asked me what was on my mind. Maybe he knew it was all terrible, unfathomable. Maybe he knew me better than I realized. And isn't that a perfect cruelty. And isn't that a marriage. Two people locked in a box together. I still talk to him, Violet, almost as much as I talk to you. Even a mouse in a trap will self-amputate rather than remain stuck, I tell him. If you'd only touched me, I tell him. All that summer I was dying over and over, I tell him, but I'm only telling the air, the empty room.

He tapped on the window again one Monday afternoon, at the same time as before, with no warning. I had just locked the door, and he watched as I came around the counter, walked over to unbolt it.

Look, I won't waste time, he said, stepping across the threshold and closing the door behind him. Would you do something for me?

All right, I said.

I want you to touch yourself, he said.

I wasn't sure I had heard him correctly. What? I asked, and he repeated his request, briskly. My eyes fixed on the pristine white collar of his shirt, I couldn't quite meet his gaze.

Here? I asked, and he smiled. A kind of acquiescence.

Go behind the counter and nobody will see, he said. I'll stand on the other side. If anyone walks past outside, it will just look like you're serving me.

I breathed in once, twice, I didn't let myself think about it. Backing behind the counter, I pulled up my skirt with one hand, and slipped the other into my underwear. I was only visible to him from the waist up. He watched me intently.

Has anybody ever seen you do this before? he asked, as if discussing the weather.

I shook my head.

Not even your husband?

I shook my head again, no.

A minute passed, another, hundreds of minutes passed, and his eyes remained in place. I moved my hand faster. I won't be able to do it, I thought, I won't be able to get there. It is a test and I will fail. I felt my face flush, while he remained cool, though he leaned forward slightly, rocking up on his feet so he could see a bit more.

You're doing well, he said. Thanks for indulging me.

I instinctively shifted my own feet a little, adjusted to give myself more support, and then to my own surprise I was growing close, my breath was quickening, and I realized he was hard, I could see him straining at his trousers, and suddenly any shame was gone, replaced by an unfamiliar and intoxicating rush of triumph.

He placed his hands on the counter, leaned forward, his forehead almost touching mine, eyes directed downwards.

Stop, he said.

Stop? I repeated, dismayed, breathless. Do you really mean stop?

Yes, he said. Stop.

I turned away from him, exposed and blinking suddenly, as if I had woken up somewhere unfamiliar. My hair was falling down and sweat stuck my dress to my armpits, making movement stiff and uncomfortable. I hoped he wouldn't notice.

Thank you, he said again, as if nothing out of the ordinary had taken place.

I waited for something more but his footsteps were already retreating, carrying him away towards the door. My eyes stung with sudden tears. I heard the door open and then I heard him pause, as if something had occurred to him. I drove past a hotel this morning, he said. On the road heading west out of town. What if we visited it?

And then I knew I hadn't failed the test.

When I got home I sat on a chair in the kitchen for a while and replayed the scene, then placed it alongside the other little betrayals, carefully lined up, carefully hidden deep in my body. I got up and set the table for dinner with a clean yellow tablecloth, then I started to cook.

The meat was ready, steaming, when I lifted the lid of the pot. As I sliced it up I pictured meeting the ambassador in the hotel room. First, he will open the door and clasp me in his arms, I decided, putting a plate in front of my husband. He will kiss the hollow of my throat very softly, and then he will gaze upon me, I decided, like he did today, but with much more tenderness. I cut my potatoes up into tiny pieces. My husband chewed and chewed, with the mouth that never kissed me. He will lay me down on the soft white bed and undo the buttons slowly, I decided. He will kiss my eyelids. I will place my hands on his smooth back, I decided as I chewed. I will clutch him to me but not too hard, not like a drowning person. The light will be dim. The bedding will be spotless. He will tell me that he has seen what nobody else has ever noticed. He will say, *It's you I've wanted all along, Elodie. I see you, Elodie. You. You.*

Dear Violet,

The man in the brown coat rang my landlady again yesterday, and once more I sat in her living room while she watched me, balefully, like I was a teenager and not a widow.

What's your name? he asked me.

What's yours? I countered, suspicious.

Auguste, he said.

Mostly I give your name if the men I sleep with ask, but this time, for whatever reason, I gave him my own.

I want to take your photograph, he said (don't laugh, Violet, I know you want to laugh), and that is how, later that day, I found myself standing on the beach in my sky-blue summer dress, my coat discarded temporarily on the shingle. The wind was hard, my arms prickled with cold.

Look straight ahead, he told me, so I stared down the barrel of the camera and kept my eyes open. I tried not to think about what I was doing. I might be afraid of being forgotten, but at the same time I do not want to leave any proof behind. I live lightly in my little room.

He didn't tell me I looked beautiful. It wasn't a seduction; I'm still not sure what it was. Nobody was watching him watching me through the lens. But I bided my time, the gulls mournful overhead, and after a while he let me put my coat on.

Try it, he said, coming towards me and handing me the camera. For once my head was empty, thoughts still. Instruct me, he said, direct me.

The machine was heavy in my hands, the strap tugged at my neck. I put it to my eye and saw him through the tiny square window, framed. He lifted his fingers up and formed an answering square with them.

I'm taking a photo of you for my memories, he said. I will remember you like this.

Cheeks scoured by wind, dark hair in his eyes, the brown coat flapping open, thick wool jumper underneath, his feet in leather shoes planted firmly on the pebbles, though they threatened to move from under him. Line of grey water behind, the faint imprints of ships.

Hold your arms out as if you're flying, I told him. Lean your body low to the ground.

He did as he was told, taking it seriously, and I pressed the shutter quick. A photograph is undeniable. I wish with all my heart I had one of the two of you together. I should have bribed, begged, stolen while I had the chance, but I never saw a single photo of you now I think about it, you had none on display in the house. I wish I had a photo of the two of us together too, maybe one from that day with the horses, on the bank of the lake, watching the children shrieking in the water. Instead I can only picture you as you must have looked on your wedding day, the chiffon up to your neck, and him, bearded and wearing a suit blacker than coal, the shirt pure white. *Click.* Or I picture you the last day I saw you, blazing and bloodstained, smiling at me from the bath as you stretched out your legs, painted toenails clutching onto the rim of the tub with strange agility, every rib stretched stark through your skin.

Now jump, I told him.

He didn't question it for a moment, just jumped on the spot, bending deep at the knee to get more lift and leaping up again with his arms still out, a tiny figure aloft inside the viewfinder.

Lie on the ground, I told him, warming to the game. I shot him from where I stood, his body prone and sideways to face me, and then I moved closer. I stood over him and took another photo that way, looking straight down at him. He was calm on the pebbles. He crossed his arms over his chest. *Click.* My fingers felt cold. I knelt down then, straddling his chest, nobody on the beach but us. I was still holding the camera, I held it right to his face, he filled the viewfinder, but he did not flinch. *Click.*

I got off him. Stand up, I said. Walk to the water.

He obeyed me at once; I followed behind him by a few steps. He didn't slow as he approached the water. I wanted to see him walk serenely through the waves, the wool coat heavy with brine, but I could not do it, at the last moment I called out Stop! though I know you wouldn't have, you would sooner have seen him drown out of curiosity than betray yourself in such a way.

Back at my boarding house, again on the stairs he walked behind me and his hand found my thigh, the smooth wood of the banister under my own hand like answering flesh, the ceiling bulb still broken and there's never anybody around so his hand moved higher, hooking a finger inside the lace of my stocking. Inside my room, he opened the curtains.

I should take your photo here as well, he said. Sit on the bed.

It was unmade, so I pulled the sheets and blankets up, pulled them straight and taut, and then I did sit on it, with my hands crossed in my lap.

Look down, he told me. Look up. Look towards that mark on the ceiling.

I raised my eyes to the rose of damp.

Now look at me, he said. He came towards me and moved my left hand to rest on my thigh, precise, my right on the bed by my side. Nobody knows where I am, he said, returning to the camera. Nobody saw me come in, nobody but you knows I'm here, these photos will be the only proof. And each of us would tell it differently, I imagine, if not immediately then in the future. *Click*. That's why I like my camera. It's objective. It provides me with a clear record, but even so, nobody will really know what went on inside this room except us, they'll only be able to infer that you sat on a bed with the light falling prettily like that, and even my memory of it will be different, I imagine, after some time has passed. *Click*. Maybe I will forget this on purpose, or maybe I will remember it for the rest of my days. It's hard to tell what an image will come to mean, what a person will mean, when you are still seeing it for the first time, and some things you always see as if for the first time.

He put the camera down and came over to the bed. The light through the window was crisp but not unforgiving. He kissed me once, formally, with his hands on my face like before. We broke away and I opened my mouth to instruct him, but he shook his head.

Let's try it differently, this time, he said.

And so, in this place that belongs to nobody, with somebody that did not belong to me, my body was touched with curiosity and with care.

Does that feel good? he asked, and I said yes when it did and no when it didn't.

Does that feel good? I asked back.

Palms pressed to chest, lips to throat, eyelids, wrists. I took to my knees, he stood up, hands in my hair, knuckles tight, he sighed and said my name, my real name, and I had not heard it spoken like that for a long time, a very long time, possibly never, and what a grief it was to realize this even in the moment that the grief was being assuaged, a need imagined and satisfied simultaneously. *Elodie. Elodie.* But beneath the pleasure, panic built in me. The old habits, not so easy to relinquish or escape. I wanted to look at my body and see yours instead, in white or black silk. The urge to speak, to demand we return to the script, was overpowering, but I closed my eyes then opened them, consciously, reminding myself. We were back on the bed. He put his hand on my face as he moved. I memorized him there, making my own image of the two of us alone in the daylight, the long brown expanse of his limbs, suddenly white at the ankle, at mid-thigh. Not a step-by-step archiving, the way I used to with you, Violet—obsessive remembering driven by the fear of forgetting, the fear of missing some crucial clue—but holding one moment lightly, like this, with the curtains moving. One frame, bordered by dark. I already knew that I would never see him again.

The Tuesday after the ambassador visited me, I baked a tart for Violet. I rubbed cold butter into flour with my fingertips, the ghost of the ambassador's hand on my waist. It might do her good to take in a secret that belonged to me for once, I thought, as I peeled and cored an apple, stinging green. We don't want to seem ugly to ourselves and even less so to those we care for, but I do believe there is an involuntary intimacy in doing the worst possible thing to somebody you love, the exquisite, weightless feeling of pulling out one of the little pins in my stomach and sliding it carefully back in. I wrapped a wine glass in a clean rag and laid it on the counter and I crushed it delicately with the rolling pin I had used to flatten the pastry, until the glass was dust. One splinter lodged in my smallest finger but it was very fine, it didn't even need dressing. I sliced the apple paper-thin, arranged it in a spiralling layer on the pastry disc, and then shook my finger over the pale half-moons. One drop fell from my flesh, leaving a faint smudge, as if I had crushed an insect. I measured sugar into a bowl, added some spoonfuls of glass and a teaspoon of cinnamon, and stirred the glittering grit around, crushing it with my wooden spoon where larger pieces remained. This I poured over the apple layer, before topping it with a pastry crust. I fashioned a tiny pastry apple complete with stalk and leaf, beat an egg, glazed it, put it in the oven. Soon it smelled beautiful. The whole tart fitted in the palm of my hand.

I took it to her wrapped in a clean white dishcloth. She ate it furtively, reluctantly, as I sat opposite her at the dining-room table. Go on, I told her when she paused. I'm not leaving until you finish. Let's get some air in here, I said once she had eaten it all, shaking out the curtains. She didn't stop me. The sun hit the table in a pool of light.

All week I waited for news of her, though I wouldn't go to her. I stood in the shop, full of desire sticky and red as berries boiled down in the pan, terrified she might be sick, and greedy at the thought too. I barely heard the people who came in, though still they spoke, still they confessed, oblivious to my distraction.

I saw a lizard eating an owl, he told me, and then the owl ate the moon.

She's wasting away, she told me. I don't know what to do about it.

I'm scared that she's starting to realize the truth, he told me.

Last night there were feathers growing on the palms of my hands, she told me.

This feeling is exhausting, she told me.

I dreamed I might be a murderer, he told me.

Yes it's wicked, but I liked it, she told me.

I drank the water of the lake, he said, and I was transformed.

I nodded, wrapped bread up in paper, let the words run off me. The men in particular were flushed in the face, all of them drinking too much. They spent too much time in the orange dusk, soaking the cuffs of their shirts in stale, spilled beer, a circle of light with the ambassador at the head, anyone passing by could see them growing strange, the half-hidden dark shapes of them. When you walked around the town, the air was electric, but only I seemed to notice. Perhaps I was even the cause of it. Every night when I closed the bakery I turned away from the window and remembered the ambassador, looking over the counter to see my hands at work, the hands that couldn't hide, unbeautiful but still so much use in them, and I touched myself again as if he were asking me and came almost immediately, I doubled over on myself and then allowed myself to fall, and on my knees behind the counter I allowed myself to weep for some time.

At church on Sunday the ambassador inserted himself next to me, where my husband usually sat. None of us commented on it, but Violet took up her usual place on my other side. As the sermon began, his leg pressed against mine, nudged harder, purposeful. Flesh braced against flesh. I recognized the scent of the ambassador's sweat from their pillows. On my other side, Violet took my hand. Her fingers went to my pulse. Your heartbeat is so fast, she whispered. You're not well. I looked straight ahead. She put her arm around me to reach him, to stroke his shoulder with her fingertips.

I tried to focus on the congregation, the rapt faces around me, the certainty of knowing everything about these lives which butted up against my own. I knew that Mme F's husband was sleeping around, for example. He was sitting quite comfortably next to his wife and daughter, though anyone watching closely might have noticed his eyes trained studiously away from a pew near the front on the left, where the mayor's wife sat, hungover, very upright. Meanwhile Josette's gaze flickered over to the grocer's eldest son from his previous marriage, though I didn't know how stupid she was being with him, had only seen him lurking in the street outside the bakery once when I returned to close up. Mme G was still locked in a feud with her neighbour, the staid and sober Mme B, over some perceived slight years ago, only mildly lessened by the recent death of Mme B's husband, and not mitigated at all by the knowledge that, during those particular years, we had all done unfortunate things. All this I saw and much more besides, but when I felt Violet's skin pressed against mine, any satisfaction related to their petty secrets left me.

The priest's voice ebbed in a dull monotone, the flowers on the altar already dead, my heart slipping out between the slats of my ribs. My eye caught on a stirring of movement in the front row, the butcher's father attempting to get up and the others around him pulling him hastily back down. But he tried again, more energetically this time, and now the ambassador leaned forward, taking an interest. The butcher's father shook off the others and sprang up, stood in the pew swaying for a moment, then pushed his way out into the aisle. The priest paused. Yes, Jean-Baptiste? he asked. The man came up close to him, as if he had never seen him before. Are you unwell?

The butcher's father turned and walked away down the aisle, staggering slightly, towards the back of the church. As he passed us I saw he was sweating profusely. His wife was hissing at him, agonizingly, to return. What's he doing? Violet whispered to me. Three rows ahead, Mme G twisted around in her seat and mouthed to me, *Drunk again*, with grim delight in her eyes. I widened my own and shook my head very slightly to discourage her. He stopped again, turned and surveyed the priest, the pulpit, the entire front pew now on their feet and helpless. And then without warning he ran, bullet-like, at the priest, who threw up his arms in defence. The butcher's father ran right past the man of God, didn't break his gait, straight to the end of the church, and he hurled himself at the stained-glass window behind the pulpit. It cracked but held, and the congregation stood up in a wave, transfixed in a moment of silent horror. He staggered back, but then before anybody could reach him he tried again, leaping, dashing himself against the shining scene, and this time the glass shattered and he disappeared. By the time I made it outside, the doctor was holding his wrist, and there was blood pooling around him, the jewelled glass everywhere, under everybody's good shoes.

We stood watching the scene for a while, and gradually the crowd dissipated. My husband invited the ambassador and Violet to join us for lunch, which surprised me, but I suppose we were all shaken, and there was a chicken to be roasted. My hands shook as I splashed the fat around with a spoon. My husband was subdued. Did he seem strange to you last night? he asked the ambassador. Now you mention it he did seem a little unwell, the ambassador replied. Violet came into the kitchen to help me serve. Sometimes reality peels back like the skin of an orange, she told me, quietly. Had I misheard her? Pass me the salt, she said.

We ate and drank with little conversation. The heat broke and it started to rain, and we lit candles. A mouse ran in, then out again. Shoo! my husband shouted. I screamed but Violet didn't flinch. Just a small thing, she said. She chewed, thoughtfully, with relish. There were no signs of illness in her. If anything she looked radiant, relaxed, as if my sharp little gift had been a cure.

My husband excused himself to use the bathroom. It felt like an opportunity, even a signal. I followed him up the stairs, telling the others I needed to fetch something. On the staircase I pulled at his shirt, pressed my fingers under the fabric. Please, I asked him. He slipped from my hands. No, he said.

He went into the bedroom, I followed him in, I put my hands on his back to feel warm skin through the cloth. Please, I asked him again. Our shadows danced around each other on the wall, I was almost chasing him around the room.

Leave me alone, he said, either in disgust or despair. Can't I have one moment without you making yourself ridiculous?

He lay on the bed with his arms crossed over his body. Please, I said again, crawling onto the bed regardless, my head dipping and brushing the coverlet, approximating seduction. He pushed me hard and I fell to the floor, stunned.

I picked myself up then and left the room, sat on the stairs for a while with my face in my hands. Below, Violet and the ambassador were talking too quietly for me to make out the words. Eventually they fell silent. I moved down a few steps and paused as the unmistakable sounds of love started. It wasn't how it was supposed to go. I crawled to the top of the stairs and considered throwing my whole body down but instead I just walked back down, loudly, taking my time over each step. Threw the door open. They were in their chairs, motionless and unruffled, as if I had imagined the whole thing. Their eyes were gleaming. Tell me a story, I asked them, sparking up a cigarette, calmly, like nothing terrible had ever happened in the world.

Dear Violet,

I wrote before that you never asked me what it was like to be told secrets. You never asked what I got out of it, and it could be that you thought it was as simple as power. But I know now that I never really had any, and I think that all those small and meaningless secrets gave me pleasure because they distracted from the larger terror of it all. They reduced it to something manageable and understandable; easier the mouthful of blood than the world in flames. If you find an explanation for the inexplicable, you might be able to stop it happening again. When I am feeling generous, I think that you two felt the terror of the world too, felt it in the same way—lodged in the gut as a cold certainty—though our reactions to it were quite different. We can be repulsed by what we recognize, as well as drawn to it. You thought I didn't see the curl of your lip when I turned around too fast, but I never missed it, Violet, and I watched with wonder how your face smoothed over instantly, easy, like water washing down a beach.

This is all conjecture. It's possible I'm being too kind to you.

It's possible I'm forgiving too much. Still, I can't get beneath your surface, I can't find your truth, even with my careful research then and since.

Were you ever really tied to the small table in the parlour with lengths of twine, wrapped around your body three times? Waiting there, naked, except for your bridal necklace. *What will be done to me. What do I want to be done.* The light of the day leaving the room. He returned fully clothed, strong arms sleeved with twill. The twine cut into your skin but left no mark. Did he ever run his hand down your flank, circle your hip bone with his thumb? Then, slipping his hand lower, hands big enough to span your waist, hands to pull him through the lake, while he dreamed all the while of pulling you through an ocean, of holding you under the water until your body was electric, dancing?

Or did he ever sit you across the dining table, put an apple on your head and throws darts at it? No, that's wrong, that's from somewhere else. We know he's unoriginal, we can laugh about it now, it's our only power, loving him and also finding him pathetic, drunk on the idea of kingdom, but he's not *that* unoriginal. All right then, did he really sit you down across from him at the dining table and raise the kitchen knife, and tell you to copy whatever he did? Then him, holding out his hand and nicking his little finger, a tiny cut, nothing to it, while you copied him with no reluctance. Did he start to cut himself deeper with solemn, easy motions, his hands and then his arms and then his torso, and did you comply each time, growing more frenetic, until the tablecloth bloomed all over with red? Did you send the tablecloth to Mme G with the rest of your laundry that week? Or did we wash it together, side by side on our knees in the lavoir, until the blood was gone? But now I think the blood was never there, your skin unbroken, just one finger hurt, a tiny bandage on your left hand that I noticed when I saw you the following day, when I clutched your hand in mine.

Or maybe he put a hot ribbon around your throat and pulled it, tight, until your head came off, and he put the head on a silver plate and lipsticked your mouth with great care, the way he had seen you do so many times. Or maybe he removed your heart with a surgeon's flourish, spent some time dissecting it to excavate what was beyond him. Or he broke your ankle, left you stranded in the room with fruit sliced on a plate, a convalescent's meal. He didn't do it under the water in the bathtub but rather bided his time, twisted your foot one morning, without warning. Small and gnarled and ugly in his hand, like a tree root or a newborn. Maybe you tried to walk but could only lurch across the room, sprawling out on the floor, but then the next day you were in the bakery as if nothing was wrong, in little blue shoes with straps tight at the ankle. Did I really pull you onto the counter in front of everyone, did I make you lie down, palm flat on your abdomen to keep you still, put my head between your thighs, put my hands around your throat, and afterwards push bread soaked in milk past your lips and teeth until you had to either swallow or suffocate, *Body of Christ?*

What if I had hit you across one cheek and then the other, would you have given me that little smile of yours, not your public smile but that little involuntary flicker, without warmth but with certain relief, certain curiosity? A smile like that of a bad child poking at a bird with a broken wing, a smile delighting in weakness wherever it might be discovered. Yes, I saw that in you. Yes, it's funny the things we remember, what leaves an impression—or maybe it's not funny at all, a smile is just the movement of the lips, you could have twitched them for any reason, your head might have been empty. You might not have thought of me at all.

I picture you waiting, always waiting, for him to come up the stairs. Breath held. He brings you a glass of red wine, and you drain half of it. Go easy, he says. He lounges on the bed, watching you seated at the dressing table, drawing yourself, but now you're too self-conscious to continue, he never watches you like this—anything else is fair game, but not these little drawings. You finish the wine. Sorry for putting you off, he says, mournful. But I brought you a present. I couldn't wait any longer.

He opens a cloth bag and pulls out a whip with several tails, the size of a small mop head. You want to clap your hands, but you restrain yourself, move to the bed, lying down and pressing your face to the coverlet, the magic already running through your veins.

And when the first blow hit, what did you feel? Did you feel replete in yourself, the undeniable fact of a body, or did the pain cleave that body from you? Did you feel that you deserved it? Was it punishment, gift, or both? A trail of fire against your skin. Could you have come just like that? I still envy you this, the reliable formula of pleasure, the satisfaction of knowing that one action would lead to another, and that way take you somewhere else. I picture your fingers curling on the bedspread, you presenting one leg and the other, your back. *Harder*, you think, but do not say. Did you look to your hands and see them feathered, clawed, a new strength coursing through you? Did you feel the cool air of the snow-capped mountains, hear the nuns reciting their litany from a distant room? I picture him helping you up, inspecting your pupils, though whether dilated from pleasure or medicine, he can't be sure. What do you see, he asks, as if you are a visionary. Tell me everything you see.

I have lost so many hours, days even, to remembering these

moments that I never lived. I am not afraid to nose around in your slick red lungs if the mood takes me. You told me, so calmly, that you wanted him to fuck you until you died, and how possible it seemed when he gripped your chin so that you couldn't break your gaze away, when you felt his teeth through his lips and afterwards you were both stunned, like two survivors of an accident. Could it have really been that way? I still want to believe that it could. Colour bursting behind your eyes when you finally dared to close them. The smell of his skin filling the room. When you came there was a clean break in your thoughts, a pure white zone of light, as if you had been beheaded. You had been looking for this feeling your whole life. You knew already that it would leave you. I wonder if you are looking for it still.

These things happened to you, not me, and though I know it's all smoke and mirrors, and though I know you were the one who lived it, the edges get smoothed over, sometimes, in this little room by the sea. If what never happened and exactly what happened can knock up against each other in this room, if we can't agree on the sequence of events, if we can see things that aren't there and remember things that never happened to us, what's the difference, really? It didn't happen to me. I make it happen to me. What's the difference, I tell myself again and again. It exists as much as it ever did. Like a memory or a rumour is something that lives of its own volition, passed from ear to ear. Waiting to be tried on, altered, archived. I picture him, picturing you. Good, he says to your body, which is never really my body, as you lie there, limp. He runs his hand down the curve of your hip and then against the ridge of your collarbone, his fingers dispassionate, as if making a calculation or taking your temperature.

My stolen memories of your life reach back into the distant past, far before I ever met you. *Stolen* is wrong, really, you gave them freely, though perhaps you didn't know what I would do with them. I think of you burning your hands on your cup of coffee in that café alone, before him, tracing your fingers in the spilled sugar all over the table. Blood in your mouth when you brought a fingertip of sweetness to your lips, knocking the coffee into your saucer, a shaking hand, catching yourself and raising your head up high. The woman at the bar kept an eye on you, she wanted no trouble, drying the glasses one after the other with that rough green cloth, so absorbed that she dropped one and it shattered, because there was something about you, something about *this woman*, with her hair tied up and her eyes like holes in her face, the gleaming gold fish in the filthy tank slithering around each other like lovers. And then he found you, he had sniffed you out, sitting so still in that frame of light, in front of the street where others passed, too fast, in their oilcloths and umbrellas. The woman at the bar watched him enter, and saw how you would give yourself over to him that afternoon in your little room that smelled like turpentine. She thought of how predictable it was, but how there was a comfort in that too.

What does it feel like to be found in that way, to have somebody walk into your life, put the money down on the table and say, *Come on*, or did he say, *Let's go*, or did he say nothing at all, did he sit momentarily and give an account of himself, did he threaten or bribe you? Were you afraid, secretly, were you hoping, secretly, that he would take off your head, take the decision away from you? All we can be sure of now is that there was a split in your life, a before and an after, and so to a studio with its rose of damp on the ceiling and hotplate and single bed which is also the room of a girl in a school in the mountains with the clear air outside the window—and his hands inside you on the dark stairwell with the broken light before your key was even in the lock, your bodies speaking a language that had called to the other through the city, and you thought about nothing, there was nothing to think about, for the first time in your life you knew what it was like to be all flesh and nerve and breath, all presence.

We don't all get those kinds of stories in our lives, Violet. Mine have never been like that. But would you like to hear them anyway? You never asked me about them when we were friends, but perhaps you're ready to listen now. I could tell you the story of the boy from the kitchens in a restaurant where I worked one summer, the summer when I could no longer be at home, so I went to a seaside resort not dissimilar to this one, and he saw the new wildness in my eyes and the beginnings of the ragged hole in my chest and he fucked me one night in the narrow bed of the dormitory I shared with other waitresses and shop girls, also being fucked around me, and I did what was expected of me or so I thought, allowed myself to be flipped over, me and the other girls stifling our voices with pillows and our hands, and he refused to acknowledge me afterwards, and afterwards my cheeks were always burning when I carried out the plates of bread and soup and frites. Sometimes I would run out and be sick, secretly hoping it was a pregnancy so that he would be forced to reconsider, he would be forced to make me a bride and that would be my revenge.

Or I could tell you about the hours I spent trying to rinse the taste of blood from my mouth, forgetting the painful lowing sound of the cows in the barn next to my parents' home, the houseful of my siblings asleep and rosy-cheeked. The story before the boy from the kitchens, which I couldn't tell you then and I won't tell now either.

The kitchen boy laughed about me with his friends. It hurt me but it also taught me that humiliation can make you feel alive, it can make you come alive. Though you can't be indiscriminate, you can't keep heaping shame upon yourself and expect to get out intact. I've learned that too now, though I didn't know it in the dormitory and I didn't know it years later either, standing in the shadows with my husband at my shoulder, watching you and the ambassador and the shapes your bodies made together. Once upon a time it seemed like marriage could be an antidote to these feelings, but what I know now is that marriage is mainly a test to be failed. And so what was I expected to do? What was left for me to do, Violet?

What I am trying to tell you, I think, is that I have been the most myself in these moments of shame, drawn inexorably down into myself, everything in my body in alignment. What I am trying to tell you is that when you finally get your face into the dirt, it can feel like a relief. I know it wasn't like that for you. Shame was another dress you tried on, discarded, lavish in your waste, a curiosity to be played at. It meant nothing to you. I didn't understand that for a long time, but I know it now, here, in my little room by the sea where the truth comes to me in waves, as the pieces fall with determination into place.

The following Saturday found me in the foyer of a nice hotel out past the edge of town. It was all arranged. I was wearing the blue dress that she chose for me; underneath it her own stockings, unwashed, tight across my skin. It was oppressively warm and muggy, threatening thunder, not that it would matter inside. The polished desk, the small yellow flowers on the wallpaper, the woman telling me that she would send my husband up when he arrived, a thin smile. My voice shook slightly as I ordered a bucket of ice and a bottle of wine, and the woman didn't comment, though it was not yet noon. There was a moment where I faltered, almost walked out. But desire retuned me into the present. The scent of my perfume rose from my neck in a hot rush. Key in hand, I walked down the thickly carpeted corridor to the room where it would all take place.

In the hotel room I took off my dress, examined how the little-worn girdle from years ago tugged me in at the middle, examined the long piece of flesh that was my body, and I felt hope, and I felt contempt, and mainly I felt grief at the waste of all the years, how much my body could have been touched, and yet how rarely it was touched. Perhaps the years should have preserved me like a thing in a museum, but bodies don't work like that; if a body isn't touched it falters faster, the yearning is visible at the surface, much as you might try to hide it. I felt so unreal there before the mirror, realizing again and again where I was with a jolt. I put the dress back on and concentrated on the last steps of my transformation—applying Violet's lipstick, re-fixing her stockings, neatening my hair. At a knock at the door I dropped the lipstick, but it was only the wine and the bucket, two glasses resting on top of the ice. And then everything was in place, and I allowed myself a smile.

Lying on the bed with my eyes closed and arms spread out I ran through the script, which I had fine-tuned so carefully over the last days, every detail polished. Yes it was predictable, the procession of touch leading to another touch leading to another touch, and that reassured me and shamed me too, how little imagination I had when it came down to it, how despite the fathomlessness of human desire I really wanted not much more than the kiss in the hollow of my throat, the dress unbuttoned with chivalry, the arms of the man slipped out of gabardine sleeves and the jacket hung nicely on the back of the chair. *It's you I've wanted all along, it's you I've noticed*, I murmured, tunelessly, *ever since I saw you in the window*.

I got up. There was no watch on my wrist and no clock in the room but I had passed a clock in the hall, so I stepped out to see the time, which was past when he should have arrived. All right then, I said to myself, late but not too late—perhaps there was a herd of cows on the road, perhaps there was a tree trunk blocking the way, perhaps there was a problem with the car, a gasket blowing with a sharp plume of smoke. Perhaps it was her, I thought, demanding something, clawing for his attention as if she could sense it was elsewhere.

Back in the room I poured myself a glass of wine, drank it in one go. I thought of all the other things happening around me, outside the sealed space of the room, which would never give up the secrets of what I did inside it. In the streets of our town and the next town and the town after that, people would be walking around as if it were any normal day. People sweating against the soil, people sitting in light-filled rooms and elbow-deep in sudsy water, violent tenderness when I thought about my husband in the bakery and the serenity with which he shaped the loaves, not imagining me here, not suspecting, pure of heart, and the bread was being sold and broken and eaten with appetite and gratitude and indifference, and everything went on. Sudden homesickness for the plate glass through which the world is neatly framed, the smell of the yeast, the small domain in which all can be achieved, the apron which is always clean in the morning. But I would return there soon, I told myself—I was just taking a little holiday. I was just taking what was owed to me, at last.

I checked the clock again and I thought for the first time then that he might not come at all. That he had meant a different hotel, or that I had misinterpreted his offer in the first place, or even that Violet might come to the door in a quiet rage, ready to exact revenge. Part of me wished for this last option. I thought she might hit me in the face, tear at my hair, then forgive me, kiss me lightly on the temple, kiss me on the mouth, cool breeze of her skin, fingers light at my waist. Lead me to the bed, allow herself to be led. I should touch myself, I thought, there on the slippery satin of the bedspread. Use the time wisely, be wet and helpless when he arrives, offer my desire up to him. But instead I paced. He won't come, I thought again, now terrified. He won't come. And if he won't come, it's all over for me.

I paced in my high shoes, coltish, absurd, I was only ever a step away from stumbling.

He won't come, I thought, pouring another glass of wine. I didn't want to go out into the hall where the clock would tell me more time had passed, so instead I lay on the bed with my eyes closed and recited the script again, but it wasn't working, the images wouldn't come any more. I sat up and drank the rest of the wine and then I smashed the empty glass against the table, not brave enough to break the bottle itself, but wanting to make some kind of gesture.

All right, I thought, stepping over the broken glass, leaving the room. All right then.

I asked the woman at reception to call me a taxi. Did I imagine her laughter, covering her mouth with her hand as she used the telephone? In the cab I gave Violet's address, panic and the need for comfort drawing me back to her like she was a lighthouse, drunk on the wine I had paid for and consumed alone. I knew I had sinned but it was not too late to atone, to slip back into her orbit, to confess to her, for a change, and be forgiven.

On the journey, the town was quiet. A lone man weaved down the pavement, almost fell over in the road, and I envied him, wished to be drunker still. Across the midday sky, a flock of pale geese flying elsewhere; I envied them too. But the sunlight on the river was still beautiful, at least, still pricked me with pleasure to see it. I was humiliated, but I wasn't dead yet.

The door to the house was unlocked and I found her in the kitchen, sitting on a wooden chair with a glass of wine on the table in front of her. She was still in her nightgown, but she seemed calmer than I had seen her for weeks. She looked me in the eye.

Hello, she said, raising the glass. What a nice surprise. Excuse me not being dressed, I'm enjoying a slow start today. Would you like a drink?

I nodded, relieved, and she got up and padded over to the cupboard. But when she stretched up to reach for a glass for me, I saw blood on her gown, thin streaks on the ivory silk. She poured me a glass and handed it over, caught me staring. Is something wrong? she asked.

You're bleeding, I said. Are you hurt?

Yes, she said, shifting suddenly, composure giving way to fear so fast she seemed like another person. She put her hand to her chest. Elodie, please help me. You're the only one left.

I watched her face crumple; guilt rose up through me in a nauseous wave. What else could I do but lead her to the bathroom, supporting her form as she leaned heavily against me. She watched as I ran the taps, hot but not too hot, and she stepped in, sat down, allowed me to lift the stained fabric over her head. Underneath, she was completely naked. I washed her so carefully with a cloth, with hot water, as she sobbed into her hands. The tiles cold under my knees, the marks on her skin red, pink, some older and scabbed, only one still bleeding. I hesitated for a second before pressing my lips to the one that seemed most healed, right at the top of her back, the investigative blow I think, when he was deciding how much she could take. A long wound, like she had been caught on a bramble. She tensed slightly at the feel of my lips and her sobbing stopped. Instead she hissed almost inaudibly, with what I still assume was pleasure. She was facing away from me, my hands on her shoulders, her dark hair dampened slightly. I could feel a new and tense energy coiling in her muscles.

You can't do that, she told me, her voice decisive suddenly, the tremor gone, while my lips were still pressed to her skin. I've thought at times maybe we would fuck, she said. But I've decided it's not for us.

Oh, I said. I took my hands off her, picked up the flannel and rinsed it carefully.

We will never do that, she said, more animated this time, forceful even, and then calm again.

I nodded though she couldn't see me, my stomach hollow.

My wine was finished, so I took her glass instead, hands shaking. I drained it and as the last liquid vanished I saw something at the bottom of the glass. A single blue bead. She turned to me, her cheeks still wet, but smiling widely now. I fished it out and held it in the palm of my hand. We both looked at it.

I know you love me, she said.

She said it like it was the only fact in the world. I closed my eyes, felt something fall inside me, let it break. Opening my eyes, I clapped my hand to my mouth, held her gaze as I swallowed the bead whole.

My nightgown, she said, standing up.

She pulled it on over her wet body and stepped out of the bath, dripping everywhere. She walked wordlessly away and I followed her, into their bedroom where I had been so many times before, the room where things did happen, had happened, would happen again, perhaps to me this time, as participant and not observer, there in the slice of light, waiting for her head or mine to be taken off. I understood my whole life had been leading to this. The curtains were shut and in the dim light we stood facing each other. Water dripped from the ends of her hair, the hem of her gown, and pooled on the floorboards.

Then she said, You really went, didn't you. Oh Elodie. You really went to the hotel. You really thought he would turn up.

She looked to the clock on the wall, eyes widening in sincere wonder. And you stayed for quite a while. Poor Elodie. I didn't think you would actually go. I thought, if not for me, then for your own dignity. How could you be so stupid?

Her tone grew dreamy. We had some fun thinking about it. We wondered whether he should go and tie you up and leave you in there until someone found you. Or bring your husband along to see you waiting there for another man. In the end it just seemed simpler to abandon the whole thing. We assumed you would know better, that some tiny instinct for self-preservation would take over in the end. But we forgot how pathetic you are. We didn't account for that.

Violet's eyes stretched wider and wider, her irises glowing like a nocturnal animal's, and the room dimmed around them.

Why? I asked simply, my throat dry.

She smiled at me. Elodie, I've been sick of this stupid town from the moment we arrived. How everybody looks at me. The least I could do was try to enjoy myself. There wasn't a great deal of enjoyment in my life for a while, you know. Things were really quite unpleasant. And you were just so willing. I could see it a mile off.

Her face was cold and glittering. The world was dropping away under my feet. She pointed at the bed. Lie down, she said.

I'm going, I said, knowing that I wouldn't.

Her voice became soft, coaxing. Look, Elodie. It's simple. You want what's mine. Don't you? Don't you want to feel what I feel, after all your listening and imagining? Because I know you do that, I know you drink it all up. You've come this far. Why not see it through?

The room was starting to waver and I was somewhere far above myself. As I lay on my back I saw her draw the whip out of its cloth bag. She ran the leather fringes lightly over her fingers, trying to catch my eye, but I moved my gaze resolutely to the ceiling, I wouldn't give her that satisfaction.

Roll over, she said, all business now. And pull your dress up.

Despite everything I obeyed her, slid onto my stomach, face down. The smell of her on the sheets overwhelmed me. I pulled up my dress to my waist and she sighed, and I flinched when she touched me, but it was just to pull the fabric up further, and then to undo the hooks of the girdle so that it fell open. I had forgotten about that, stiffened under her hands.

Don't be shy, she said, soothingly. We've shared so much. Believe me when I say there's little I haven't seen. She patted me encouragingly. Next time you try to fuck my husband, though, I'd get new underwear. You look awful in this. I'm not sure he would even have been able to get hard.

Cool air from the window on my naked back, my dress bunched around my shoulders. I heard the blades of leather cut through the air and then immediately they licked the skin of my back sharply. I moved like a cat in water, shocked by the pain, but then I forced myself to lie still again, wanting to like it. Wanting to understand. But it was just pain after all, ordinary pain, like the time I had accidentally leaned my arm against the stove as a child, a sewing needle thrust unthinkingly into the skin, a horse blamelessly crushing a foot. I wanted my mind to be a glowing line of white light. *Harder*, I thought, wondering if that was the key—if that was where rapture lay. I had faith in my body's capacity for resilience, even if for nothing else. There was a lot I could take. I listened to her pause, presumably examining my back, taking aim.

She hit me again, much more forcefully, and again I recoiled and clenched and bit down on the bedding, and again I waited for transformation. I waited for my skin to fall from me in ribbons and for somebody else to be revealed, but there was only more pain, deeper but somehow even more unremarkable than before, and this time there was also grief that the pain revealed nothing to me, that perhaps there was nothing to be revealed at all.

She hit me again, one last time, not quite as hard as the previous blow, as if she was tired or even bored. And there was nothing except the sting, and the heat, and I let out a small, choked cry, and that was it.

She came to the bed, turned my head to the side so I could see her face right next to mine, lips almost touching.

Three blows, she said, counting them on her fingers. One for each of us—me, you, and him. Three blows for the woman who watches everything and sees nothing.

I flinched, and she pulled me closer.

Listen, Elodie, this is important, she said. She looked into my eyes, tapped my nose with her finger, and I focused on her sharp teeth, the movement of her lips as she spoke, glimpses of the dark back of her throat.

The woman spied on two strangers at their own bedroom door and she was bewitched by them. She befriended them, husband and wife. She haunted their home, stole their possessions and ate their food, swept their floor and breathed their dust. She was poisoned by envy at what she saw, betraying the wife again and again, even though they were supposed to be friends. Her eyes grew larger and more covetous day by day because everything she saw, she wanted for her own.

Violet smiled. She watched the strangers so closely that she did not notice her own husband. She did not see her own life at all.

Because the baker had a secret too. There was a baby planted like an apple pip in the stomach of another woman, his true love. And he planned to leave with her, to seek a life of happiness far away from the woman with enormous eyes and an empty heart. And in time the strangers will leave too, they will travel onward, but the woman who watched from the shadows will stay here forever.

I lay on the bed, motionless before her, saw the blue-veined breasts of the grocer's wife at the lavoir, slipping Violet's clothes over her softly swelling form. I thought of how kind she had been to me recently, how gentle. I thought about her down in the baking cellar on midsummer eve, bright-eyed, not minding the heat.

Violet watched my mind racing and she smiled wider.

Three blows to remind her who she is, that underneath she is nothing, not a great duchess in her castle or a secret agent or a damsel waiting to be rescued, nothing of the sort. Nobody knows what will become of her, and nobody cares. Nobody cares about the stranger either, the wife in the house alone, envied and despised by the town, but happier than any of them. Nobody cares about her, but she doesn't care about any of them either. Violet dropped her voice to a whisper. She cares least of all about you.

She rose to her feet as I wept, and stood beside the bed like a visitation. She seemed invigorated by my tears. I sobbed and sobbed, curled up, newly aware of the pain at my back, the blood flowing. She put her hand on my bare shoulder. There you are, she told me. She kissed me once, precisely, on the soft blade of the bone.

I don't remember leaving their house, don't remember whether I walked calmly down the stairs or ran. I do remember a rising commotion coming from the main street as I slipped down the back roads behind it, blood seeping through my sky-blue dress, the sounds like the market setting up, except it was a Saturday so that couldn't be right. I do remember that the bakery was closed unexpectedly, the door locked when I tried to open it, though Josette should have been there. My husband should have been there. Maybe he was with the grocer's wife, I thought. Maybe they had already gone, left while I was waiting in the hotel, outwitted by everybody who was supposed to love me. I would have to go home, anyway, I told myself. There was nowhere else to go.

I came back to a house as dark and silent as the bakery. Upstairs my husband was in bed alone—naked, sweating, his hair plastered to his face.

Water, he rasped when he saw me. I had to close the bakery, I feel terrible. His eyes became wide and strange. Where have you been?

His unfamiliar intensity confused me, he who was always distant and cold. I came closer to the bed and he groped for my legs.

Please, he said. Help me.

I backed away, went to the bathroom and wetted a washcloth, filled a glass for him to drink, sponged his face.

How long have you been like this? I asked.

His clothes were all over the room. He started to babble, his hands out in front of him as if throttling an invisible enemy.

How long? I asked again.

I don't know, he replied, momentarily lucid. After breakfast.

The room flickered around me, blinking out then returning in sharp focus, too sharp. Still drunk from the wine in the hotel, the wine Violet gave me. I tried to concentrate.

(Meanwhile, the ambassador coming in the door as quietly as a thief, coming up the stairs to find her motionless in the bedroom, looking out of the window. Perhaps he took her hands and kissed them.

It's time for my medicine, she told him.

You don't have to take it any more, he said. You're cured.

No, she said. I want my medicine—and he smiled and smiled.

Out in the street, a new sound was building. He took a vial from the bedside cabinet and told her to open her mouth, so she closed her eyes and stuck out her tongue and felt a single bitter drop sliding down her throat, and she waited for one reality to end and another to begin.

Let's go out and explore, he said. They left the house together in high spirits, almost laughing, walking fast. And as they moved down the street the whole town was transformed before their eyes, the weary stones made new. A town unpeeled.

How do you feel? he asked.

So happy, she told him. So happy to be here, with you.)

Dear Violet,

I don't know how much you know of what happened after I left your house that last time we met. Not all of it, I'm sure. Though it stands to reason that you witnessed some things first-hand. Some things I remember, some I was told by the doctors, some I have read in the newspaper, or gleaned from chance conversations, unexpectedly. Some things I have admitted to the police, not all. Even now, a flash of colour can recall something: a face, a movement, a cry. The curtain lifts up then falls again. Shall I tell you what happened, Violet? Shall I tell you the story?

The grocer went first, taking a knife to his own heart the way he opened up the goose on Sundays. A steady pressing towards the ribcage, the point searching for where the bone is weakest. It takes a lot of force to cut through bone, the strength of somebody already outside of their own body. His wife watched him in horror, both hands on her belly. She had thrown up her breakfast that morning and felt quite normal. Later she would tell the policemen that she screamed (*What else would I do?* the witness told the officers), yet when I picture the scene now I can't imagine her doing that. I imagine her standing quite calmly, taking it in. A new development, this husband opening the shirt and feeling for the beat of his blood, rib and sternum, the shirt only just put on, washed just days before at the lavoir in anticipation of an unremarkable week. There is always someone there, afterwards, to make an account of your tragedy: *The patient inserted the knife into his chest.* But I think this is a scene that deserves the colour, the details, like the knuckle of bread left on the table, the spill of milk from an unsteady hand, the light of a day outside which promised to be beautiful, the curve of her stomach, the stone of the wall against her back, and the answering curve of her body, as she shrank away from the scene. He was dreamlike, sedated, unperturbed by the horror of the witnessing party, his wife, and the un-witnessing parties, including the baby in the stomach, including me. *The patient opened his chest and severed the organ from the surrounding tissue,* as transcribed by the coroner. He pulled it out with his own hands. There it was, on the table, like it was such a simple thing to do all along.

Mme G threw herself down the stairs, trying to get away from a demon, wine-red and shining. She turned around on the landing and there it was, come from somewhere, from a dark corner or the fireplace, and so she made one long, instinctive leap, the most graceful movement she had managed in years. Afterwards she was conscious and not in pain, somehow, though she couldn't move. Crumpled on the flagstones she watched the light skittering, shimmering, in tiny yellow squares against the wall. She couldn't see the demon any more but she could sense it pacing at the top of the stairs, snorting like a horse, trying to find a way down to her. There was a grim satisfaction in her superstitions finding fruition. Come and get me then, she thought, though when she tried to shout the words they would not come out. Just try, and we'll see who wins this time.

When I rang for the doctor there was no answer. I watched my hand grow smaller, then larger. I closed my eyes, told myself it was the heat, the heat playing tricks. The shock of an imagined life, carefully nurtured, being torn down. The shock of a real life being turned inside out. Both are survivable. My husband moaned. And I remembered the unlabelled glass bottle, placed on the table between us. *Give us this day our daily bread.* What have you done? I asked him, urgently, but he only moaned louder. I went back downstairs and studied the crumb of the bread, and I thought it did seem paler, but none of the colours were working anyway and the ground tipped again. On the table, sugar spilled from where my husband had made himself coffee, a broken cup in the sink, and when I spun around to confront the man watching me from the corner of the kitchen it was my father, and I sunk to my knees, my heart mangled under the weight of what is recognized and not recalled, he shrank back and became nothing but paint. It's not real, I told myself, I returned to the stairs clutching the loaf, still, and a bowl of milk, slopped it over the edge and onto the steps as I climbed, vertiginously.

Three houses away the mayor was being eaten by snakes. He could hear his own voice, unbearable in his head, shouting for help as the serpents writhed in his stomach, eating their way out, but he was just whimpering and nobody could hear, not even his wife, who was turning on the taps to see fire dripping out. She watched curiously, switched them on full. Sweat beaded against the mayor's bald head, his red shirt torn open and his hands, frantic, dragging at his skin, nails leaving long marks. He wanted to pull the snakes out, tried to put his hand down his own throat but could not get far enough to reach them. So he tried to vomit them out, got onto all fours and tried his hand again, bucking his body. His wife was hypnotized by then, trailing her hands in the cold fire, overflowing to the floor where it set everything alight painlessly. She remembered, dimly, how an errant shell had destroyed the old church, and then she was back there, waiting for the fire to subside, picking wailing through the rubble to find the dead, searching for days.

Why did the ambassador take you out that afternoon, Violet? Why did he lead you by the hand into what he knew was waiting? Did you feel once more the way you did the first time you met him—following, trusting, relieved? I suppose I can understand that he needed to see it, what he had done. He should have planned it better, should have left the town with you before the first bread was broken, but he wanted to see it up close. Did he know it would be like this? I can almost picture him with notebook and camera, dispassionately recording the scene for men an ocean away, men in expensive suits for whom we were purely theoretical, a small town with a thin skin barely healed, and underneath it our wounds still pulsing, crawling with life. A town of no importance. But to take you with him into that scene. Maybe you insisted. Maybe witnessing the pain of others made you, temporarily, forget your own. Even our puny pain, which you held in such contempt. Blood scattered your front step. Did it help to see it? Yes—I believe it helped a little.

So the story continues. You know this part already. He took your hand again, and you walked like that through the streets. You passed women and men with slick, red hands. A broken shop window with the glass watery on the ground, the contents—bolts of cloth, buttons, spools of thread—strewn everywhere. You could hear sirens in the distance, guttural sounds coming from the open windows and doors of the houses you passed, and you clutched at the ambassador's side, exultant still. A man, I still don't know who, started to scream from an upstairs window, there were engines in his lungs and he was growing wings and he was going to fly away into the clouds, and you felt a jolt of recognition, Violet, I imagine.

I see it, I see it! he shouted.

He took a step and launched himself into the sky, and for a second you thought he would make it; that the air would sag under his weight and then he would rebound, up and up, he would leave this place, he would leave it lightly. Instead he fell to the stone pavement, legs first. The ambassador approached him and the man screamed, batted him away.

Leave me alone! he cried, red blooming through his trousers. I'll try again!

The two of you continued down the street, more quickly. You saw communion everywhere. Your heart was inside out, worn redly on your blouse for everyone to see.

Police from the next town were on their way by then, and the ambulances too, tearing up the road. Not everyone had eaten the bread that morning. The doctor had rushed out the door without breakfast to treat a man whose walls were speaking to him. He rang the hospital, except upon leaving the man's house he was immediately accosted, dragged into another house, and then he knew something was badly wrong. Those who did not or could not eat stared at their family members, who were shucking off their skins. You are dead, Mme A told her elderly mother, the woman who had spent ten years in the feud with Mme G. The matron sat in the rocking chair and waved her hands, tapped her feet, took her own pulse. I'm not dead, she protested. You are dead, her daughter repeated, starting to weep. You died in the explosion. We laid you out in the back room. Her mother breathed against the palms of her own hands, found a small mirror and breathed against that too, showed the cloud to her daughter as proof, but still the daughter backed away. You must go, the daughter told her. You have to go back, you can't be here. She shut herself in a cupboard, sat down among the damp-smelling cottons. Mme B tapped on the door, once, twice, three times. Took her own pulse again.

Josette, who had started to hide her bread underneath her bed each morning out of fear of her growing body, watched in wonder as her parents started to break every plate, every bowl, in the house. They threw them on the floor, where they shattered, until the ground was thick with ceramic shards. They walked around with bare feet, unfeeling, trailing blood, looking for more things to break. She ran into her younger brother's room and found him sitting on the edge of his bed, staring into space. When she called his name he looked at her as if he didn't know her. She called it again and again, *Oli*, his childhood nickname, not used in years, and with that he sprang up and his hands were around her throat, she tried to scream but there was no breath in her, there was only the superhuman strength of her brother who was only just a teenager, who was shy and liked birds and got excited when she brought home stale bread from the bakery for him. Afterwards they found red crescent welts on her skin where his fingernails had dug in.

I left my home. As I locked the door it grew soft, my hands sinking into it. The world was too beautiful to be believed. On my hands and knees I crawled for a while, occasionally vomiting into the gutter. Someone ran past, their face twisted like a dishcloth, and I reached out my hand, but they did not stop. I tried to walk again, one step at a time. One, I told myself. One. One. Steps that led to nowhere, steps forgotten as soon as I took them. The patch of sky above me, framed by the pale stone buildings, was irradiated blue, and it distracted me, pulled me in.

The butcher stood in the cold store among all his meat, and watched with curiosity as the animals started to sway, releasing themselves gracefully from their hooks. The suckling pig, the calf split right down the middle, the little rabbits with their paws up as though begging—they circled him slowly, walking on their hind trotters as though they were feet, as though they had been doing it forever. He took up his cleaver and swung it at their gleaming and bloody figures, but they were too nimble, they danced right out of reach. The cleaver hit the thick stone wall and chipped, again and again. It was the pigs that began to sing first, an icy but familiar song, and though he couldn't quite place it, it made him drop the cleaver and put his hands over his ears and sob.

You and the ambassador were running by this point, through the winding streets, the smell of smoke, your feet pelting against the ground. The people around you called out for help, hanging out of their doors and crying and bleeding, and you did not stop, did not even think to stop. Is this where it changed for you both— where the fun ended? Perhaps by then the ambassador had stopped smiling, perhaps he stopped smiling when he heard the crack of bones in the man who thought he could fly, undeniable like a gunshot. Perhaps he thought with the first stirrings of fear about the true meaning of the word *experiment*—the unpredictability of what he had unleashed, and the power of it. The elegy for an entire world, rising up from our throats in a wail, whether we were low to the ground beneath a terrible sky or busy dying inside, feeling our minds slip through our hands at long last.

The streets were closing around you too tightly and you were running for the church, where no harm could come to you. *Body of Christ*. In the graveyard it seemed that the dead were rising from the earth, but you blinked and looked again and saw it was just the living, clutching at tombstones and covered in soil, bewildered to find themselves there. Inside the church you stumbled to the front. Did the light shine unbearable over the font, streaming through the broken stained-glass? The window was boarded up with cardboard but it couldn't cover the hole entirely. He pulled you down in the second pew, hidden from sight. With the stone warm against your knees, did you think again about your wedding day, walking down the aisle towards him, this man holding your hands in his? Did he seem real to you, finally?

I find myself wondering now whether our reactions were unique, Violet, or whether every town would erupt like that when the switch is flicked, when reality is peeled back like the skin of an orange. Would it have happened regardless, sooner or later, with or without the ambassador's interventions? The recent traumas still too close to the surface, too many things to be forgotten, though how we tried, everything terrible still happening, over and over. The air shimmered with gold. A brick came through a window of the church, then another. How much did you understand of it, Violet? How much were you in on it? I want to believe you were innocent, I really do. I want to believe you were a victim as much as the rest of us, but how can I know, after what happened between us.

This is how I transformed, in the end. My clothes torn. My cells altering. I noticed a cluster of children's faces like ducklings watching from a window, crying, remembered dimly having given them slices of cake, sugared brioche, in another world. I ran and ran, faster than I had ever gone before. When I kicked off my shoes I saw my feet transform into hooves and I was ecstatic. In my new body I could outrun anything. I could outrun the disappointments, the grief, outrun past and present both, cast off these things with hot, unspooling energy. I could run towards beauty itself, become beauty itself, better late than never. I ran past the monstrous crowd, pushed against flesh with my hands and everybody moved out of my way, miraculously dissolving; ran past the sun gleaming on the river; ran towards the sound of the sirens, feet bloody by that point but I felt nothing, cheeks burning red and I felt nothing. Ahead of me the men with the nets they used to catch the stray dogs, and I had barely understood what it meant before I was caught, upended, the ground at my face. Warm dust, bitten lip, wet and bruised and unrecognizable.

It's gone, I said, when they crouched down to question me. Everything is gone.

Or that is what I am told I said. I remember my lips moving. I remember the dust. I remember and then it vanishes, it comes back in the night sometimes, or when I am on the beach, my hands in the sand, and suddenly I am insensible, there is such a grief in the world cracked open, one reality ending and another beginning, and no way back for any of us.

Are you still listening, Violet? Would you tell me your side of the story if you were here? Would you tell me to stop ruminating, to stop tripping myself up—tell me I should know better, I'm still alive after all, waiting in my little room, and the grey streak of sea outside which will be there forever, which will outlast everything.

They came looking for you in the church. Of course they did, because the town was fine until you arrived. That's a lie—it hadn't been fine for a long time, but none of us could admit that. Things knitted along, things worked as much as was necessary, and we told ourselves it was enough. And then there you were, the two of you, arriving one night in the pouring rain for a reason nobody knew, and afterwards nothing was the same. You can't blame them for dragging you from the pew. You can't blame them for carrying you in their arms, like you were being worshipped or celebrated. They left the ambassador sprawled in the aisle, kicking him so he wouldn't get up. One man couldn't do this to a whole town. But a woman like you, with your long dark hair, and the marks on your arms and ankles. I picture them tearing off your dress, how they hissed to see the welts on your back, your ribs standing out.

They bore you towards the river, hands clutching around your limbs. The men with the nets were too far away to stop them. Did you fight, Violet, or did you go limp? What did you see there, waiting for you in the water? Perhaps the river would boil, perhaps you would shrink into a bird and fly away, perhaps you were as curious as anyone to know what would come next. Perhaps it was a relief. The mystery of the world laid out for you in vivid colour, one last time.

I believed for a long time that I had had a cat named Minou, that she had slipped through the earliest years of my childhood like white smoke. I recalled the scratch of her claws and the weight of her on my baby legs. It turned out there had never been a Minou, that for years my memory of that was unreal. And yet she came back to me in the hospital, once only. She was sitting on Violet's lap, in a chair at my bedside. I was drugged to the hilt and never wanted it to end, if it would mean the two of them would stay there beside me, peaceful, for the rest of my life. The purr like machinery. Her hands still on pale fur.

Wool-wrapped days, white light, something injected in the arm.

The newspapers gave me her full name. She was once a child like everyone else, born to two people in a country that was not mine. She grew up in that green place, got older, and then she went away. She was never married to the ambassador, after all. The wedding she described was an elaborate fantasy of her own. It might have been one she told for the pleasure of lying, or one she wanted badly to be true. In fact, the papers made no mention of the ambassador anywhere. She bears it all—the terrible blame for being a certain kind of woman. Some of the more lurid tabloids even speculated she was having an affair with my husband. *Star-crossed lovers of Hell!* went the headline, with an illustration of the devil himself holding a baguette, cartoonish and leering. None of the stories ever mentioned me.

The women from the lavoir return to me too, sometimes. It started in the hospital, where they would gather around my narrow iron bed, and they have followed me here. At first I wished they wouldn't, but now I understand. They don't want to be forgotten, and they don't mean any harm. I am the one left alive. I am the archivist, the keeper of their secrets. They gather around me with wet cloth in their hands, drowned cloth, marked with blood that won't wash out.

The ambassador rescued her from an asylum.

No, it didn't go quite like that.

She orders her groceries in hampers from the city.

Crystallized fruits, tins of olives, truffles. Yes.

She was a whore.

Sometimes.

She bathes in milk and rose petals.

Not that I ever saw.

The bakery was sold while I was still in hospital—my sister's husband organized it, though he struggled to find a buyer for a while. The town cycles through bakers quickly now; they do bad business, they are mistrusted by those who remain, but there is always someone desperate enough to take their chances when the job opens up again. Gossip travels this far, tells me of the red paint flung on the door that I used to unlock daily, the plate-glass windows smashed more than once. I picture the grocer's wife pushing her baby, who might be my husband's child, to the bakery in the pram. There always has to be bread; the idea might sicken her, or might have sickened her at first, perhaps it took her a while to take that first bite, but who does she think she is? What else can she possibly do. The child that saved her life waving his little hands for a morsel, and her scooping out the soft middle for him to mash between his gums.

Meanwhile, at the seaside, the gulls still throw shellfish on the floor, clams plucked from the shoreline. The memories are losing their power, the police are growing bored. They came to me to tell me they were closing the case, and I made them the usual black coffee in the two cups I own, and sat and watched them drink it.

But who will stand trial, I asked.

There's no one to blame, they reassured me. Just a bad batch of flour. It wasn't your husband's fault, we're sure of that. It could have happened to anyone.

The officer who I think of as kind took my hand in his. I hope this gives you some peace. We're sorry for your loss.

But what about the ambassador, I said, unable to contain the secret any longer.

Who?

The American. The man who lived with Violet.

The less kind one raised his eyebrows fractionally. Yes, the ambassador. Several of your neighbours mentioned him too. But there is no record of an American man of his description living in the town last year. He glanced at his colleague as if for support. We'll leave you to your rest now, madame.

Since then there have been no more phone calls for me. Just like I predicted, Auguste has vanished; I knew it in the cinema when he told me that an image was just a moment. Sometimes I think he might have been right after all. That without proof, without anything to touch or hold on to, forgetting will happen one day like waking up from a dream, only traces left, puzzling even to myself. One day the twinned violence that issued from Violet and the ambassador might feel far away. The poison they fed us, each in their way. Was it just the same old game of follow-the-leader? Or did she know then what we know now, was she driven wild by what we chose to forget, that the world is only ever one breach away from being unpeeled entirely, one tragedy, one glimpse behind the curtain. I still see so clearly the light in the café on the day she met him. The window shining out a perfect square of warmth and Violet there at the table, stiff and upright as if waiting for someone to take off her head. She is not there any more but she is also always there, spilling the sugar over the table. I think she will be there forever. I think of her with compassion, and not just because I know she would hate that. The truth is that I've seen behind the curtain too, I realize now I saw behind it long before they arrived, and the possibility of transformation, that destruction which can feel a lot like peace when it comes, was in me all along.

Dear Violet,

I am learning that the unexplainable moments can be the most beautiful ones of all. These things seen and not-seen, things heard and misheard, the flimsiness we build entire lives around. Perfect bread, a man who wanted to start a new life, a town bewitched. The ordinary and the sordid nestling together.

There is one last memory. One last thing to be told.

It goes like this: I stagger up the stairs, drugged, reeling, and set the bowl of milk, the bread, on top of the chest of drawers in our bedroom. I watch my husband writhe, and think about him sitting with the ambassador in the orange light, beer sticky across the tables, the brandy being poured. I imagine him telling the ambassador about his problem, the bread that is always the same, the wife made of salt, another man's wife at his door. I think about how desire grows in the spaces around the known, where things are at their most and least real, where the terror of all the possibilities fracturing out through our lives is suspended, momentarily, so we can look them in the eye for once, and isn't that what we are searching for when we debase ourselves for love, one moment of certainty in this strange and beautiful world. The ambassador who offered to help him with the bread, casual, confident, and all the rest will follow, leading him to that moment between a before and an after. Transformation, absolution, whatever you want to call it. I beat at my husband with my fists. He is calm and still under my blows, which are not capable of causing physical damage. My fists become hands again, smooth the hair from his brow.

You're the devil, he tells me, quite amicably.

I love you, I tell him in return.

For his own safety and mine I take the opportunity to button him up inside one of his white linen smocks, back to front with his arms tucked down inside the sheath of the body, flipping him with some difficulty onto his stomach in order to do up his buttons and tie the loose sleeves at the back—he is heavy, bigger than me, bigger than the ambassador, but he shifts obligingly as I move him—I have to stop for a moment and pant for breath and keep reminding myself that what is seen is not objective, what is witnessed is not always real, sometimes it's just a trick of the light or a wreath of smoke making it look like your head is being taken off.

With my help he moves to a sitting position, propped against the headboard. Are you hungry? I ask. I go to the chest and retrieve the bread and milk, bring them back to him and break off a small part of the perfect loaf. I soak it in the milk. Eat of it and be filled. I put the wet bread in his mouth and he chews gladly, swallows. Eat of it and be transformed. Everything is shot through with colour. If you are going to see, you might as well see clearly. There will always be someone to make an account of your tragedy, even if it is just yourself in the end, recording, noting, the crimes against your person, the various ways you have been done or undone. My father returns to the room, and my mother too, crowding the bed. They have walked up the frozen river with the rest of the dead, except they never saw this town of bleached stone and flour, they never knew me here, and so who am I to them—matronly Elodie who sees everything, who knows the power in seeing, or cringing fifteen-year-old Elle waiting in the barn, not knowing there are bigger lives, uglier and lovelier lives to come—I have not seen her in some time but I see her now, she comes back to me, she comes back through me, the shape of her like something far up ahead on a road. Far behind. Do not leave me here. I soak more bread, press it into my husband's mouth, he takes it willingly into himself. We are nearing the end of the loaf. He is full now, trying to move again, as if he is starting to burn somewhere inside him. You did it, I tell him, tenderly, putting the bowl down. Look at me. I promise you that I am here. And the energy spills out of him, crystalline, harder than sugar, more beautiful than snow.

In the summer of 1951, the small French town of Pont-Saint-Esprit succumbed to a mass poisoning. There are many theories regarding the source of this catastrophe. None have ever been proved.

Acknowledgements

Cursed Bread was written during strange times, and I am so grateful to everyone who made it happen in ways obvious and non-obvious. Thank you to Christopher Alcock for encouraging me during lockdown, and for all the happy years we have shared. Thank you to the amazing Krista Williams, Sophie Thomas, Nia Davies, and the rest of our Welsh crew. Thank you to my best boys Edward John and Luke Bell for feeding and looking after me. Thank you to all my brilliant friends, with special shout-outs to Beverley Murrow, Lauren and Jake Salmonsmith, Jess Rochman, Elisha Hartwig, Chris Talbot and Jack Gahan. Thank you to Emmie Francis, ultimate housemate. Thank you to everyone who gave me a sofa or space while I figured things out. Thank you to my family, for always being there for me.

Thank you to the whole team at Prague Municipal Library for giving me the incredible opportunity of being writer-in-residence as part of the Prague UNESCO City of Literature initiative, particularly Alena Tománková and Radka Navarova, who looked after me so well. Thank you to Freddy and

Veronika (and Iris!) for Sundays in Prague, and to Tomas Mika for showing me around. Thank you to the Irish Cultural Centre in Paris, to the American University of Paris, and to the University of Kent in Paris, for a wonderful month in France, with particular thanks to Amanda Dennis and Yelena Moskovich. Thank you to my Paris gang—Andrew, Maria, Rou, Kleo, JB—for healing chats, fun and wine.

Thank you as always to my agent Harriet Moore, whose encouragement, support and wisdom is beyond measure. Thank you to Hermione Thompson, Margo Shickmanter, Deborah Sun de la Cruz, Lee Boudreaux—my dream editorial team this side of the pond and across it. Thank you to Simon Prosser, Hannah Chukwu, Rosanna Safaty, Ellie Smith, Ana Espinoza, and everyone else who has brought this book to life. Thank you to all the booksellers and readers who have championed and supported my work—I couldn't do it without you.

BLUE TICKET

Calla knows how the lottery works. Everyone does. On the day of your first bleed, you report to the station to learn what kind of woman you will be. A white ticket grants you marriage and children. A blue ticket grants you a career and freedom. You are relieved of the terrible burden of choice. And once you've taken your ticket, there is no going back. But what if the life you're given is the wrong one? When Calla, a blue-ticket woman, begins to question her fate, she must go on the run. Pregnant and desperate, Calla must contend with whether or not the lottery knows her better than she knows herself—and what that might mean for her child. With *Blue Ticket,* Sophie Mackintosh has created another mesmerizing, refracted vision of our world that explores the impossible decisions women have to make when society restricts their choices.

Fiction

ALSO AVAILABLE
The Water Cure